DRAEKON FIRE

EXILED TO THE PRISON PLANET

LEE SAVINO

LILI ZANDER

Many thanks to Miranda for her sharp eyes.

Cover Design by Kasmit Covers

DRAEKON FIRE

Crazy jungle planet. Killer orange fungus. Crimson snakes in the water. The worst part? While I was in a coma, I seem to have acquired two dragon mates.

When I wake from my coma, the first thing I see are two hot aliens.

And I'm informed that they're my mates.

I don't think so.

This isn't the story of Sleeping Beauty, and the two sexy, possessive, Draekons aren't my fairy tale princes.

I'm certainly not going to wake up, kiss them, and live happily ever after on this stupid prison planet, where everything's out to kill me.

Not happening.

Not even if they heal me from my injuries and nurse me back to health.

Not even if they protect me, care me, and keep me safe.

Not even if their abs could grace the cover of every men's fitness magazine back home.

Sleeping Beauty isn't going to kiss her Draekons. She's going to find a way back home.

Draekon Fire is the second book in the Dragons in Exile series. It's a full-length, standalone science fiction dragon-shifter MFM menage romance story featuring a snarky human female, and two sexy aliens that are determined to claim their mate. (No M/M) Happily-ever-after guaranteed!

THE DRAGONS IN EXILE SERIES

Are you all caught up with the Draekons? Don't miss any of the books.

*The **Must Love Draekons** newsletter is your source for all things Draekon. Subscribe today and receive a free copy of Draekon Rescue, a special Draekon story not available for sale.*

THE LOWLANDS AND SURROUNDING AREAS

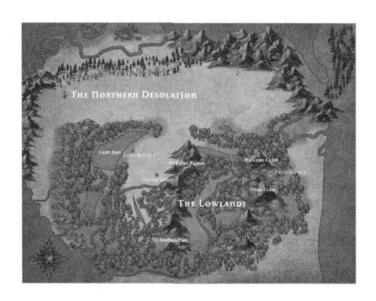

PROLOGUE

Raiht'vi:

The winds are howling when I wake up at the crack of dawn. The twin suns, Paarun and Vaarun, are barely visible, obstructed by the swirling sands of the Natal.

At my side, the other apprentices still sleep. I savor the precious moment of peace and quiet. When the three girls wake, the subtle torments will start anew. Broken beakers, ruined experiments, and snide insults about my lack of family—Kal'vi, Noor'vi, and Ashl'vi are envious of my skill in the lab, and they seize every opportunity to express their jealousy.

If only they knew who I really was.

I'm in my third year of a ten-year apprenticeship. The path to becoming a scientist of Zoraht is long and arduous. In the first year, there had been fifty of us. That number has already been winnowed down to thirty. My father assures me that no more than five will don indigo robes at the conclusion of our training. "Of course, you will be one of them," he says to me, a forbidding expression on his face. "Won't you, Raiht'vi?"

My path has been determined for me from the moment of my birth, and I won't shirk my duty. "Yes, father."

I get dressed and head downstairs to the large labs. In our third year, we've moved on to self-directed projects. I'm working on creating a disease-resistant fungus that can be made into high-protein rations for the Zorahn soldiers. My father had sniffed disapprovingly when I told him about my project. "We have the ability to create new races of sentient beings, and you want to feed the army?"

Vasht'vi, my instructor, is more encouraging. Today, she looks up at me with a smile when I enter my laboratory. "I've been looking over your notes," she says. "I think you're almost there."

"Thank you, Scientist," I murmur. Vasht'vi is sparse with her compliments, and her words of praise are few and far between.

"The other apprentices dream of glory," she says curtly. "They dream of creating races as powerful as the Draekons and the Paarons, but those breakthroughs are rare, even for the White Ones. You are smart to pick a project that you can succeed at."

I'm not unlike the other apprentices; I too dream of glory. One day, I intend to be one of the white-clad scientists. There are only thirteen living men and women that have earned the honor of wearing the ivory robes. My heart's ambition is to join them. My father earned his robes when he was sixty; I will do it sooner than him.

"When you have finished today's experiments," Vasht'vi continues, "clean your space and follow me. You'll be working in the underground levels from tomorrow."

My heart leaps in my chest. The lower levels are

reserved only for the most secret experiments, for the most talented scientists. "Thank you, Scientist," I stammer, too overwhelmed to be able to express my gratitude appropriately. "I won't let you down."

Her expression turns grim. "I argued against it," she says. "I think you have too much promise to get tangled up in the work they do down there, but the decision wasn't up to me. The order came all the way from the Head of the Council."

My mouth goes dry as Vasht'vi's words sink in. It isn't a compliment that my father thinks I'm ready for the underground labs. *It's a test.*

"I hope you have a strong stomach, Raiht'vi. You're going to need it."

VASHT'VI WASN'T LYING, I reflect two weeks later. Nothing in my training has prepared me for the perversion, the utter awfulness of the underground labs.

We are scientists of Zorahn. We create life. *Not in the underground labs.* Here, under the guise of understanding Draekon physiology, we seek to destroy.

The woman on the examination table flinches as I draw near. "Please," she begs, her voice cracking with desperation. "Highborn, I beseech you. Please don't hurt me."

I can't look at her. My eyes slither away. "I'm just getting a blood sample," I say quietly. "It won't hurt you. The wound will heal." I can feel the gaze of the other apprentice, Travix, on my back. I know he thinks I'm too soft with the test subjects, but I can't forget that they're people.

People who aren't here voluntarily. People who are being tortured in the name of science.

The woman has been kidnapped from the streets of Giflan. That's bad enough, but the man lying next to her?

He's a soldier of the Empire and judging by the tattoos on his flesh, he's high-ranked. Even Travix had paled when he'd seen him for the first time. The soldiers report directly to the High Emperor. For the scientists to kidnap one of them is to declare war on the Zorahn Empire.

I didn't realize how deep the vein of ambition runs in Brunox's blood.

Every scientist knows the story of Wonacx, the Head of the Council who thought he could control the Draekons. The tale doesn't have a happy ending. The Draekons rebelled and broke free of their long enslavement, and Car'vi, the beloved daughter of the High Emperor Kannix, had been killed. In his anger and his grief, Kannix had ordered Wonacx's death.

If Dravex were to find out what we are doing in this underground lab, my father will be executed.

I slide my needle into the woman's veins and draw blood. She whimpers as the clear tube pierces her skin, and she turns her face away from the sight of the bright blue liquid filling the beaker. Squeamish. I used to be like her once.

The soldier next to her stirs and moans. He's been unconscious every time I've been in the lab. I don't know what kind of tests they're performing on him, and I don't have the nerve to ask.

"What are you doing?" Travix asks me curiously.

"Comparing the Draekon mutation in her blood to his," I reply, nodding at the two subjects. "According to the Book of Wonacx, the Draekon males morph into the dragon when they glimpse their mate."

"I've read it," Travix replies smugly. "The Draekons mate in a triad. Where's the third?"

I repress the urge to roll my eyes. How did one so dense

as Travix make it through three years of apprenticeship? "If the three are united," I say through gritted teeth, "the males will transform into dragons." I nod to the soldier. "We've been experimenting on that man for months. How do you think the High Emperor is going to react when one of his Zoraken tell him about this lab?"

Travix looks chastened and leaves shortly after. I work in silence, uninterrupted. Day turns into night, but I pay the lateness of the hour no mind. The problem I've been tasked with—figuring out why Draekons shift when they lay eyes on their mate—is one that has eluded generations of scientists. Though I feel singularly unqualified for the weighty task, I know better than to question my assignment.

I'M FALLING asleep at my desk when the alarms go off. Deep gongs sound through the Crimson Citadel, their tones warning of an unexpected visitor.

A black-clad guard bursts into the laboratories. "Highborn," he says, bowing to me. "Vulrux, Thirdborn of Zoraht, is in the citadel, and he's making his way underground."

Fear grips my heart. Vulrux is young, but already, he's causing waves in the Saaric by speaking up against the scientists. "Where's Vasht'vi?" I ask the guard. "Or Norlux? Any of the other indigo-clad?"

The man shakes his head. "Everyone's left for the night, Highborn. Only the apprentices are left in the citadel."

"Bast," I swear, my thoughts racing. Vulrux can't see me here. The Thirdborn has never met me, but once he sees this lab, he will stop at nothing to uncover the truth. I'm the daughter of the Head of the Council. My presence in this space incriminates my father.

I put down my beaker and whirl toward the exit, making

my way to the safety of the observation rooms. From the windows there, I watch the scene unfold.

Vulrux bursts into the laboratory like a man on a mission. When he catches sight of the two prisoners, he goes still. "What does this mean?" he asks the guard at his side, his voice dangerous. "Who are these people?" He notices the male's markings for the first time, and he inhales. "Is that a soldier of the Empire? Do the scientists dare experiment on a Zoraken?"

The situation is spiraling out of control. Vulrux has recognized the soldier. He cannot be allowed to leave alive. If he carries word back to the High Emperor of what we do here, it will be the end of the scientists. "Where's Brunox?" I demand sharply. "Summon him. Now."

The guard at my side looks grey-faced with fear. "Word has been sent, Highborn."

I turn my attention back to the Thirdborn. *Just in time.*

Something is happening. The air goes still. The hair on my skin rises as I watch. Vulrux's eyes meet the woman's, and he drops to his knees, his face contorting in pain.

The soldier flexes his muscles, and the straps binding him to the examination table snap. I watch, transfixed, as the haze shrouding his eyes clears.

They both speak as one. "Ours," they growl. "Our mate."

Then they transform into dragons.

The guard next to me gibbers in horror. Thankfully, the others in his unit are made of sterner material. A commander appears next to me, seeming to materialize out of thin air. "Highborn," he says. "What should we do?"

Why are you asking me, I want to cry out. But I know why. I'm Highborn, and I'm the senior-most apprentice in the building. Everyone else is in bed, or home with their families.

My father isn't here. To save us all from his reckless machinations, I must act.

My thoughts race. I think of everything I've read in the ThoughtVaults, every forbidden word I've pored over in the Book of Wonacx. Draekons are not easy to kill. Once they possess the power to transform at will, we have no weapons to destroy them.

Forgive me; I have no choice. "Tell your men to fire at the woman."

The soldiers obey. I watch, frozen in horror, as the woman crumbles under the assault. The two Draekons cry out in pain as she dies, and my gamble pays off. Vulrux and the unnamed soldier transform back to men.

"You've done well, Raiht'vi."

I've waited so long to hear words of praise from my father's lips, but when they finally emerge, I'm too numb to respond. "What will happen to them?" I whisper. "To the Thirdborn and the soldier?"

We can't keep them here now. They are too dangerous. Anything might trigger the shift. Though the prevailing wisdom is that the second shift happens when the Draekons claim their mate, I don't trust it. The only thing that we know for sure about the Draekons is that we can't predict them. Their genes constantly mutate in the face of threats.

"Exile," Brunox replies.

It is a better answer than I hoped. The prison planet is a death sentence, but not an immediate one. "The Firstborn will ask questions if his cousin disappears without a trace." It is widely known that Arax, Firstborn of Zoraht, is closer to his cousin Vulrux than he is to his own brother Lenox.

"It will be handled." My father's expression is forbidding

and doesn't invite any further questions. I don't push my luck.

When you kill an innocent, you stain your soul. Today, I killed that poor woman in the underground labs. One day, in the gardens of Caeron, I will hold up the fabric of my soul, and I will be judged for my crimes. Until that day, the look of anguish in the eyes of the Thirdborn and the soldier will haunt me, as will the sound of the nameless woman's voice pleading with me. *Highborn, I beseech you. Please don't hurt me.*

Dennox:

Once again, I watch my mate die in front of my eyes, and once again, I'm helpless to act.

A dozen people are clustered around Harper Boyd's bedside. The human woman has been in a coma for twelve moons. She breathes on her own, and when we hold water to her lips, she drinks. But she hasn't eaten in twelve days. Her body wastes away to nothing in front of our eyes, and there is nothing any of us can do to stop it.

"I'm completely out of ideas," the human healer, Sofia Menendez says, a frustrated look on her face. "Viola, any thoughts?"

Viola Lewis, the human mate of Arax and Nyx, shakes her head helplessly. "I've got nothing." She turns to Vulrux. "Tell us again what happened to Rorix. How did he come out of his coma?"

"The situations are nothing alike." I speak for the first time, my voice harsh. The Firstborn looks up, surprise on his face at my interruption. Too late, I realize that no-one knows why I'm drawn to this human woman's bedside. No-one knows that Harper Boyd is my mate.

Except for Vulrux, Thirdborn of Zoraht. My pair-bond feels the same complex set of emotions that I do. Vulrux is a healer who couldn't save his mate. I'm a soldier who couldn't protect her. Our shame is etched deep into our souls, and we've never spoken of the events that led to our exile.

"Rorix was in a waking trance," I continue. "He didn't speak, and he didn't appear to recognize us, but he still ate and drank." I take a deep breath. "This human woman is frail. She isn't Draekon. She doesn't have long to live."

Viola Lewis has a stricken expression on her face at my words. Ryanna Dickson, a dark-haired human woman, straightens, her eyes flashing with anger. "Harper isn't frail," she says tightly. "She's not helpless, and neither are we. If there is a way to save her, we will find it."

Nyx puts his arm around his mate and gives me an annoyed look. "Even the thieves on the streets of Vissa learn tact," he bites out. "It's a pity that the Zoraken aren't taught manners."

No. We're taught instead to kill.

I stare back at Nyx, refusing to back down. The thief has never lost a mate. Who is he to speak to me of tact? Has he lived through the pain of watching two mates die? Has he ever felt as helpless as I do at this moment? I am cursed by the lives I've taken, and the fabric of my soul lies in shreds. That must be why the fates taunt me so.

"Enough." Vulrux steps between the two of us, his voice calm. "Our arguments do not help Harper Boyd."

He's right. Unfortunately, we're out of ideas. Vulrux has tried every medicinal herb in his stores on the human woman. Sofia Menendez has given her drugs from her meager supplies. Nothing has revived our mate.

Slowly, the others trickle away. I stay where I am, ignoring Arax's thoughtful stare. When I'm alone with Harper Boyd, I lay my hand over hers. The woman's flesh is hot to the touch, her skin the color of an angry sea. The toxin lingers in her blood, but unlike the mild venom of the *kilpei* plant, it can't be sucked out.

When Vulrux had carried her up the cliffs on his back, unwilling to entrust the precious human to any of the others, our mate had been wearing the strange clothing of her people, a dark blue garment that clung to her body, highlighting every curve. Now, she's got a towel draped over her, the thin silvery fabric made from the sturdy webs spun by the *ahuma*, and nothing else. The dragon inside me purrs at the thought of her nakedness and demands I complete the mating bond, but I am Zoraken, and I have honor. This woman is more than a soft body. She is a person with thoughts and wishes of her own, and whatever her dreams of her future were, I'm sure they didn't involve being stranded on an alien planet and dying from a poisonous fungus.

"Harper Boyd," I say softly. "I was a soldier of the Empire. I killed in the name of the High Emperor, and though the mind-wipes prevent me from remembering everything, I know that my soul is stained and tattered." I take a deep breath. "The Zoraken do not take mates. We do not have families. We die in battle, and I have no cause to expect more."

Yet I do.

She stirs in her sleep, and I tense, hoping against hope that she will wake. Vulrux must sense her movement because he reappears at her bedside. His shoulders slump when he realizes that she's still unconscious. "Nothing?" he asks me.

I shake my head.

"The first time," he says quietly, "I was young. I had lost before I knew what loss was. This time—" His voice trails off.

I seldom let my thoughts wander to the time I was held captive by the scientists. There was a woman there, but the dragon within me hadn't recognized her as my mate. Not until Vulrux had shown up to complete the triad.

It was the same way when Vulrux had set this human woman down on his bed. The instant the three of us were in the same room, the golden bonds had brightened, but they'd faded almost immediately.

Harper Boyd is dying.

"You are both fools." A harsh voice interrupts us. I look up to see one of the scientists in the doorway. *Raiht'vi.*

Every time I look at the white-clad woman, animosity rises in my blood. I've searched my memories—those still left to me after repeated mind-wipes—and I can't recollect her. Then again, the images in my mind are fragmented, a result of the cocktail of drugs that have been forced into me from the time I was conscripted.

"What do you mean?" Vulrux's voice is mild, but I sense the tautly stretched anger underneath.

"You think with your hearts," she snaps, moving into the room. Her steps are slow, and her face contorts in pain as she moves. She is still healing from her wounds, but that doesn't stop her from glaring at us. "Try using your minds instead."

"You speak in riddles," I say icily. "Explain."

"Before the Zoraken, there were the Draekons," she replies. "They were the perfect soldier race. They were made to be invulnerable." She stares at me with a strange expression on her face. "You are Draekon, soldier. The poisons on this world cannot harm you. Pass that immunity on to your mate."

Our heads snap up in shock at her words. "How do you know that Harper Boyd is our mate?" Vulrux asks, his hands clenching into fists. "No one else knows."

"Many have eyes and do not see."

I am a soldier of the Empire. I know how to *persuade* Raiht'vi to part with her secrets, but I doubt that the First-born will give us permission to torture the scientist. Besides, even though her words are riddled with mystery, she's telling us something important. "What immunity? We cannot resist the fungus any more than the humans can. Rorix was in a coma for six months."

She huffs impatiently. "The Draekons adapt. If Rorix were to brush against the same fungus today, it would give him nothing other than a rash. His immunity will have passed onto you."

My spine prickles with unease. "I don't trust you. I will not risk hurting our mate."

"Her words make sense." The human healer, Sofia Menendez stands in the doorway. I wonder how long she's been there. In normal times, I would have heard her approach before she got near, but I'm distracted by the lovely golden-haired woman next to me, her breathing labored as she struggles to live. "In essence, that's how vaccines work on Earth. I think we should try it."

"No." Vulrux's lips tighten. "I agree with Dennox. My experience tells me that scientists are not to be trusted."

Raiht'vi moves swiftly. Before I can react, she grabs Vulrux's knife from his belt and slices a deep cut in Harper Boyd's palm. Sofia shrieks as red blood gushes out from the wound. "Are you insane?" the human healer says angrily. "What have you done?"

Raiht'vi faces her squarely. "The human doesn't have time for your endless debates," she snarls. She turns to the two of us. "Act now to save your mate, Draekon. Let your blood mingle with hers."

My jaw tightens. "If this fails," I promise the crimson-haired scientist, "I will see you dead of my own hands."

She doesn't reply. She grabs the human healer by the hand, and half-drags, half-pushes her from the room. With sick fear in my heart, I pull my knife out and slice a cut in my palm. Vulrux does the same. The two of us take Harper's hand in ours. Our bright blue blood mingles with her rich red.

We wait. The moments tick by. Harper Boyd's breathing stutters and seems to cease, and time comes to a halt. I'm ready to find the scientist, wrap my hands around her throat and squeeze when Vulrux's voice stops me. "Wait."

Golden threads appear in my mind's eye, chains that bind Vulrux and me to the woman on the bed. As we hold her hand, the bonds strengthen. The deep blue poison in Harper Boyd's blood recedes, and her skin regains a pinkish hue. Her eyelashes flutter.

The beast within me exults. *Our mate lives,* it growls in triumph. *As soon as she wakes, we will claim her.*

But the beast doesn't rule me. The man does. And the man has learned that the mate-bond brings only pain.

Harper:

When I open my eyes, several realizations sweep over me, each one more disconcerting than the next.

I have no idea where I am.

Two hot, naked-to-the-waist guys are in the room with me. They're holding my hand in theirs, and as I watch, drops of blue blood spill on the silver sheet.

And I'm not wearing a stitch of clothing.

I'm not sure if I should freak out or part my legs for the hunks.

I settle for neither. Drama isn't really my style, and though I have nothing against hook-up culture, if I'm going to put out, I'd like a meal and some attempt at conversation first. In a world where courtship has been replaced by swipe-rights, that makes me high-maintenance.

Hang on, Harper. Two strange guys are holding your hand, their blood is freaking blue, and you're thinking about Tinder?

The memories slowly start to return. Alien spaceship. Crash landing. Injured Zorahns leaking blue blood. Green and blue moons, pink skies.

Viola, Ryanna, Sofia, and I had set out to find food and water so we could survive the next week until the Zorahns used their superior technology and rescued us. We were walking toward Penis Mountain, but I'd tripped, and some orange goo had tried to kill me.

Since I'm not dead, I guess I've been rescued and treated, and unless blue blood is super-common in the galaxy, the two men at my side must be Zorahn.

I look around covertly. I thought Zoraht would be filled with sleek metal and glass towers and little airships buzzing about in the sky. *Probably because I read too much science-fiction as a kid.* This room isn't very high-tech. The texture of the walls looks like wood, though the colors—pink, green, and black—remind me that I'm not on Earth. The effect is a little psychedelic. *Groovy, baby.*

The two Zorahn aren't looking at my face; their attention is focused on my arm. I'm assuming they're observing the effects of the orange jello from hell. Their expressions are somber. I swallow nervously. "Is it bad?"

Both their heads snap up at the sound of my voice. The taller and broader of the two men says something, relief etched on his face.

Unfortunately for me, I have no idea what his words mean.

Great. I've managed to lose my translator.

"Hey, buddy?" I try to sit up, and my head swims. I feel nauseous. Ugh. I hate being sick. "You know one of those golden thingies that go in my ear and shock the heck out of me? I'm missing mine. You can't rustle up a spare, can you?"

I point to my right ear at the same time. I'm being a little flippant since I assume neither man can understand me, but at my snark, both men's eyebrows rise, and an amused smile curls around the lips of the non-linebacker. He gets to his feet and moves to a corner, returning a minute later with my own personal babel-fish.

Shit. I see the golden translator embedded in his ear, and it dawns on me. I can't understand them, but they can understand me just fine, and they probably think I'm an idiot.

My cheeks heat as I reach for the little device. Non-linebacker, who has dark hair that falls in sexy, shaggy waves around his face, and vividly green eyes, doesn't hand it to me. Instead, his fingers stroke my forehead and he tucks a strand of hair behind my ears, before inserting the golden disk into my right ear.

Whoa. Tingles. Tingles everywhere as the hot alien touches me. My arm might be sore, and there appears to be a gash in my palm, but my girl-bits are humming happy songs.

Stupid girl bits. I've met Beirax, and the tall alien has a massive stick up his butt. Zorahn men might be easy on the eye—and trust me, these two are very easy on my baby blues—but fun to hang out with they're not.

I sit up, slower this time. "Where am I?" I ask them. "Is this Zoraht? Where are the others? Are they safe?"

Mr. Linebacker speaks for the first time. "Your companions are well, Harper Boyd." When he smiles at me, his caramel eyes warm and kind, my insides do a funny flip. I thought Beirax was huge, but this Zorahn makes Beirax seem puny. He's tall, broad and muscled. His chest is crisscrossed with scars, but they don't do anything to detract from his gorgeousness. If anything, they just make him hotter.

"Where's Viola?" She'd told Sofia and Ryanna to take me back to the ship, while she went to find water and food. The two women were supposed to put me back into stasis. Is that what happened? "Is she okay? Did you find her before you whisked us off the prison planet?"

An expression of consternation flashes over the linebacker's face. He looks at the other alien, who clears his throat. "This might come as a shock," he says gently. "You aren't on Zoraht. You're still on the prison planet."

My brain struggles to comprehend his words. "But why?" I stammer. "The spaceship went down. They'd have to know we crashed—they must have radar, or whatever they use in space. Why haven't they come for us? They told us we were under the personal protection of the High Emperor. Surely that's got to be good for a rescue mission."

The green-eyed alien raises an eyebrow. "Lenox's word?" His tone makes it clear he doesn't think much of the High Emperor. That's not a good sign. The other Zorahn seemed to think that Lenox was the best thing that had happened since sliced bread.

Another thought occurs to me, one that causes anxiety to rise in my chest. What had Viola said before we set out? This was the world in which the Zorahn exiled their criminals. Draekon, she'd called them.

The two aliens sitting next to me aren't Zorahn doctors. They're not to be trusted. They're to be feared.

My arm throbs and my head spins. The room goes blurry, and I fall into a dead faint.

3

Vulrux:

My throat tightens with fear as unconsciousness claims her, but our mate's breathing stays even, and her coloring is healthy. "Her body is recovering," a voice says behind me. *Raiht'vi again.* "Let her rest."

I give the woman a hard look. Raiht'vi had hustled Sofia Menendez out of the room when our mate's eyes had opened, and for that, I'm grateful, but my loathing of the scientist hasn't abated. I can't ever forget that fateful night in the Crimson Citadel.

Raiht'vi and Beirax are still recovering from their wounds, and I will aid that recovery as best as I can. When they are well, however, things will change. I will question them, and I will get answers. Sixty years ago, the Scientists' pet guards trained their weapons on our mate. Someone ordered them to kill her, and I intend to find out who that person is.

If I were not stuck on the prison planet, I would seek revenge, but I can't. The truth is all I can hope for.

You will find happiness with Harper Boyd, the beast inside me insists, but I'm not hopeful. The dragon is ruled by biology and nothing else. I saw the expression of fear in our mate's eyes before she fainted. *She is afraid of me.*

Haldax enters the room on Raiht'vi's heels, and I frown. Especially during the rainy season, when the fourteen of us are crammed together in close quarters, we respect each other's privacy and never enter another's dwelling unless expressly invited.

The rigidly traditional Zorahn gives me an apologetic look. "The Firstborn wants to talk to you, Raiht'vi, and Dennox," he says in explanation. "Thrax will guard the human woman."

I heave an inward sigh. I've avoided having this conversation with my cousin for sixty years, but I can't hide the truth forever.

"WHY DID you cut Harper Boyd's hand?" Arax stares at Raiht'vi, his arms folded over his chest. We're in the dining area. The rains beat a drumbeat on the roof, an ever-present sound during the rainy season. "Why did you push Sofia Menendez out of Vulrux's quarters? What are you playing at, Raiht'vi?"

Viola Lewis, who is sitting next to Arax, has a concerned expression on her face. Next to her are the two human women, Sofia Menendez and Ryanna Dickson.

In the ten days that my cousin's mate has been in our encampment, I've come to like and respect the three human women. They're dealing with a lot. Through no fault of their own, they've crash-landed on the prison planet and cannot escape. Half of their companions were stolen by another Draekon exile batch, and the rains prevent us from searching for them. Harper Boyd, one of their friends, has been in a coma.

Rather than fall to pieces, Viola set out to find help. Sofia Menendez takes refuge in discovering the various properties of the medicinal herbs in my stores, and Ryanna Dickson is learning how to fight with a bone knife.

It is Sofia Menendez, the human healer, who speaks up now. "Before Raiht'vi threw me out, I overheard you," she admits softly, looking directly at Dennox. "You called Harper your mate."

Arax and Nyx inhale sharply. "Your mate?" Arax says. "How is that possible? You didn't transform."

I take a deep breath and exchange a glance with Dennox. He nods almost imperceptibly. "We've never talked about the testing and the exile," I tell my cousin. "For good reason. It is a time of pain for all of us, a time when we were torn from our families. But for Dennox and I, it was more."

I tell them the story of that long-ago night. "Both Dennox and I transformed into dragons when we set eyes on the woman," I tell Arax. "But she was killed, and we were exiled, and we've never allowed ourselves to think of it. When you told us how you transformed when you saw your mate, I understood better. Both Dennox and I have already transformed once. The creature inside me was wounded when she was killed and has remained dormant all these years."

"Until Harper," Viola says softly.

Raiht'vi mouth twists. "One mating and you think you know everything about your history," she says disdainfully.

Arax's gaze turns steely. "Scientist," he snaps. "Do not test my patience with your half-truths, your hints, and your innuendos. I'm not in a mood to be toyed with. The human woman could have bled to death as a result of your actions."

"She's fine," I interject. "She regained consciousness." I address Raiht'vi for the first time. "You were right about Draekon immunity. You have my gratitude."

She doesn't meet my gaze. I don't have time to ponder why; the moment I tell everyone that Harper Boyd regained consciousness, the human women jump to their feet, joy and relief etched on their faces. "She's awake?" Viola squeals. "Can we go see her?"

Arax nods. He gives Raiht'vi a hard stare. "This isn't over, scientist." He turns to me, his expression troubled. "You kept this from me all these years," he says softly. "Did you think I would react with fear when I learned about your transformation?"

"Of course not." I lay my hand on my cousin's shoulder. "It was a painful time. My mate had been killed, and my heart lay in tatters. I just wanted to forget."

"And now? What of Harper?"

"She doesn't know us." A sense of hopelessness spreads through me. "She looks at us with fear, not desire."

Nyx steps up and says something in a low voice to Arax that I can't hear. At Nyx's words, Arax's face turns grim, and he nods tensely. "You're right," he says to his pair-bond. "But we need to wait for the human to heal."

Unease fills my mind. I don't like the way Arax is surveying Dennox and me. My intuition tells me I'm not going to like whatever he has planned.

4

Harper:

I drift in and out of consciousness for days. Every time I wake, one of the two hotties are at my side. They feed me bowls of broth and small helpings of meat and fruit, and they give me a strange green potion to drink. I want to ask them where my friends are, but I'm never awake long enough to be able to satisfy my curiosity.

Should I be afraid of them? I'm not. They might be criminals, but their eyes are kind, and they're taking really good care of me. I decide not to worry about it.

THE ROOM IS empty when I wake up. The two hotties are nowhere to be seen, and another large alien with warm, golden-brown skin stands in the doorway.

He turns around when I attempt to sit up. *Stealth warrior I'm not.* "Hi," I greet him.

"Ah, you're awake," my guard says cheerfully. He's as tall as the other two Zorahn, but he's leaner than them. He looks like a runner. "Vulrux and Dennox have been worried sick." His grin widens. "I'm going to have so much fun teasing Rorix about this."

He seems friendly, and not at all like a dangerous criminal, not, of course, that I have any way of telling. "Who's Rorix and why are you going to tease him?"

"Rorix brushed against the same fungus you did," he replies. "But he was in a coma for three months." An amused smile curls at his mouth. "You're up in fifteen days. I'm Thrax, by the way."

"And I'm Harper," I reply. "I wouldn't be so quick to mock Rorix if I were you. My body feels like an elephant has been using it for a trampoline. That's not normal, is it?"

His gaze goes distant. If I had to guess, the translator in his ear is probably explaining the concept of a trampoline to him. I wonder what he thinks of it.

I don't have too long to wait to find out. "You humans do some strange things," he says, laughter in his voice. "You jump up and down on a stretched piece of hide for fun?"

I hear voices. Before Thrax can reply, my three ladies enter the room. Viola, Sofia, and Ryanna. "Oh my God, Harper," Viola says, flinging her arms around me. "You're awake at last. You've been in and out of consciousness for the last three days, and even though Vulrux and Dennox swore you were going to be okay, I was freaking out. Thank heavens you're alive."

I return her hug a little awkwardly. "I'm pretty excited about living too," I deadpan. "But it looks like I've missed a lot. The two hunky aliens told me that we're not on Zoraht. Fill me in. What the hell's going on?"

The women exchange glances. "Thrax, could you leave us alone for a few moments?" Viola asks the alien in the room.

"Of course," Thrax replies, speaking with a deference that surprises me. Back on Earth, the Zorahn treated us as if we were beneath them. I wonder what's changed.

Once it's just the four of us, Viola sits down on the mattress next to me. Sofia and Ryanna perch at the foot of the bed. "Don't freak out," Ryanna warns me. "You're not going to like this tale of woe."

"What do you mean, don't freak out?" I ask cautiously. Something's afoot. Thrax said I was in a coma for fifteen days. What's been happening while I've been unconscious?

Sofia gives Ryanna an irritated look. "Look what you've done," she scolds the dark-haired woman. "You're worrying Harper."

"Actually, all three of you are," I reply. "Whatever it is, just spit it out. I'm a big girl. I can take it." Something strikes me. "Where are the others, by the way? Olivia? May? Are they still in stasis?"

Viola doesn't meet my eyes. "They're fine. We think." She draws a deep breath. "Okay, it's rip-off-the-Band-Aid time. The last time you were conscious, we were trying to find food and water so we could survive until we were rescued, right? Well, here's the thing. There's no rescue possible. We're stuck on this planet forever."

"What?" My voice comes out in a thin shriek.

Almost immediately, the two aliens who have been taking care of me enter the room. "Are you okay?" Linebacker asks me, his voice gentle. "Do you need anything?"

Fuck yes. A brand-new, shiny spaceship that has the power to get me the hell away from this hot, humid, planet, filled with poisonous fungi that want to kill me. And, while we're wishing for things, a bar of chocolate would be nice too.

Viola sighs. "She's fine, Dennox," she says, her voice tired. "Can we talk to Harper in private for a few minutes?"

The other alien gives Sofia a questioning look. "Viola just told Harper that we can't leave the prison planet," she explains. "She's fine, Vulrux, I promise. I won't let her get too tired."

Vulrux and Dennox. Those are the names of the two aliens who've been taking care of me. Dennox is the linebacker, and Vulrux is the green-eyed one who eye-rolled at the idea of the High Emperor helping us.

Vulrux gives me a questioning look, and I nod slightly. "We'll be right outside if you need us," he says.

The two of them leave. "Explain," I tell my fellow astronauts, my head spinning with confusion. "What do you mean, we're stuck here?"

"An asteroid belt surrounds this planet," Viola replies. "No Zorahn pilot can get a ship through it without serious damage. You saw what happened to the *Fehrat 1*."

"Okay." My mind feels fuzzy, but I focus my thoughts as best as I can. "How did the eye-candy get here?"

Ryanna snorts in laughter at my description of the aliens. "The eye-candy," she says, "were put in a drone ship." Her lips tighten. "The Zorahn weren't very concerned with their survival."

Her comment prompts another thought. "What did they do?" I ask curiously. "Why were they exiled to this world? They aren't serial killers, are they?"

Viola shakes her head. "They're Draekons," she replies. "Men that can shapeshift into dragons. They were created by the Zorahn scientists to be soldiers more than a thousand years ago, but there was some kind of rebellion, and they were all killed. Ever since then, the Zorahn test their population yearly, and when they find someone with Draekon genes, they exile them. The fourteen men in this camp have been here for sixty years." She smiles faintly. "Obviously, the Zorahn live longer than humans."

I barely register Viola's comment about how old the aliens are, and I even ignore the fact that they can shape-shift into dragons; I'm so shocked by the circumstances that led to their exile. "Wow," I murmur, horrified to my core. "That's shitty. How do you know all this?"

"She's banging two of them," Ryanna replies with a grin. "They shifted into dragons when they saw her. They're her *mates*."

To each their own, I guess. I'm not going to critique Viola's taste in men. I'm more concerned with the 'stuck on this planet forever' situation. "Can we fix the spaceship? Or their drone ship, can we MacGyver it to get us out of here?"

"There's a big hole in our hull, Harper," Sofia says. "Remember?"

"Holes can be welded," I retort. "Between their ship and ours, maybe we have enough parts to get one useful spaceship."

From the look on their faces, I'm assuming they haven't thought about it. Frustration rises in me. It sounds like in the two weeks I've been doing my best Sleeping Beauty imitation, these three have resigned themselves to living on this hellish planet for the rest of their lives.

Scratch that. Sofia and Ryanna might be resigned to living here, but Viola is captivated, from all accounts, by dragon dick.

Not me. I'm not giving up without a fight.

"I can't believe," I say acidly to Viola, "that you've just assumed we have no options. Where's your backbone? You're going to stay here and play cavewoman with your two aliens, and forget about your life back on Earth?"

"I didn't have a life back on Earth," she retorts grimly. "Besides, what makes you think that going back is a good idea, even if it were possible? Our government sold us out to the Zorahn with no due diligence. Do you trust the Zorahn scientists to keep us safe? Arax was the Firstborn, and they exiled him. What kind of protection do you think we'll have?"

I think of the way Vulrux had rolled his eyes when he talked about the High Emperor. Maybe Viola's right.

Then my natural skepticism reasserts itself. "Hang on. Fourteen men were exiled to this planet. Suddenly, nine women show up in their midst. Of course, they're going to tell you whatever the fuck it takes to keep you here. As far as they're concerned, Christmas came early. They're not going to give us up."

Viola's lips tighten. "I trust Arax and Nyx," she says. "I believe them. They're not lying when they tell us there's no way out of here."

"What about the others?" I demand. "Olivia, May, Felicity, Paige, and Bryce. Where are they?"

Sofia answers me. "They were taken by another Draekon exile batch," she says unhappily. "We're not sure if they are prisoners, or if they're there of their own free will."

I try to jump to my feet. Bad mistake. The room spins around me, and I collapse back on the bed. Thankfully, my two Draekon protectors don't hear me. "They're what?" I screech. "And you're sitting here instead of looking for them?" I glare at Viola accusingly. "You're having sex while the others are being held captive?"

Viola turns white. Ryanna puts a hand on her shoulder. "There's nothing we can do, Harper," she says. "It's the rainy season. It's coming down so badly that you can't see your hand in front of your face. Can't you hear the deluge?"

Now that she mentions it, I notice the dull, pounding throb on the roof. "That's rain?"

Sofia nods. "According to the guys, it goes on for three months," she says. "You remember that mountain we were walking toward when you got poisoned? We're at the peak of that mountain right now, and the lowlands surrounding us are flooded. We can't do anything until the weather improves."

"Not even Viola's pet dragons?" I snap. "They can't fly on recon missions and find our friends?"

"Why don't you go outside and see for yourself?" Viola snarls, pushed too far. "Maybe then you'll realize that while you were unconscious, we weren't idle. We're trying to figure out how to survive here, Harper, and your crappy attitude isn't helping."

She seems on the point of tears. As if they sense her emotions, two new men enter the room and move to her side. I'm assuming these are Viola's dragons. Their lips tighten when they take in Viola's distress. "*Aida?*" one of them says softly. "What's the matter?"

I feel a slight tinge of envy when I see the way the two of them look at the brown-haired botanist. As if she's the only woman for them. Back on Earth, I'd hoped that Tom would look at me that way.

Of course, Tom had turned out to be a two-timing weasel, and he'd been such a dick that I'd had to quit my job. Running out of money, I'd volunteered to travel to an alien planet.

Now, I'm stranded.

Viola smiles tremulously at the man who asked her the question. He's got shoulder-length dark hair, and a beard covers his face. "Nothing," she tells him. "Harper was just concerned about Olivia, May and the others."

Shame trickles through me. Viola could have tattled on me, but she's put the nicest possible spin on my yelling spree.

I don't think Bearded Dragon believes her. "I'm Arax," he says to me. "I'm the leader of this exile batch." He indicates the man next to him. "This is Nyx, my pair-bond. Nyx, will you fetch Vulrux and Dennox? We have something to discuss."

I happen to catch Viola's expression. She's biting her lower lip, and she looks nervous.

I don't have time to ponder what's going on because the two hotties re-enter the room. Vulrux's eyes fly to Arax's face and his body tenses. "What are you planning, Arax?" he asks bluntly.

Arax doesn't answer him directly. He turns to me. "Harper Boyd," he says. "You've already met Vulrux and Dennox. Their blood mingled with yours, and it saved your life."

"Yeah." My throat is dry. I can't help feeling like the other shoe is about to drop. *Any moment now.* "I'm pretty grateful."

"Vulrux and Dennox are your mates," Arax continues. "Your presence wakes the dragons inside them."

Wait, what? No, no, *hell no.* Viola might be happy to shack up with her hot alien lovers on this planet, but I'm going back to Earth, where we have things like cell phones, Internet access, and pizza delivery.

I'm not the only one who doesn't think much of this mating thing. Viola's looking pole-axed, and both Vulrux and Dennox have identical unhappy frowns on their faces.

Huh. I'm pretty glad the aliens aren't itching to jump me, but I can't deny feeling a little wounded pride at their disinterest.

"We need all the strength we can muster to find your missing friends," Arax says. "If Vulrux and Dennox complete the mating bond, there will be two more of us that can transform into dragons."

Viola bites her lip. "Arax," she says quietly, "we can't force Harper. That's not how we do things."

"No," Arax agrees. "I won't compel anyone to mate against their will." He straightens. "Here is my decree. Vulrux and Dennox, you will court Harper Boyd. You will spend your waking hours together. If by the time the rains cease, the three of you are not bonded, you are free to go your separate ways."

"What the fuck, Arax?" Viola demands. Got to give her credit, she thinks this idea is bullshit as well. Complete, total bullshit.

"Vulrux and Dennox will not force Harper Boyd," he replies, as if that's all that matters. "But if we are to save the other women, I need Draekons who can transform at will." He gives me a hard look. "I heard you earlier," he says to me. "You seemed very concerned about the fate of your companions. Here's your opportunity to demonstrate your caring."

He spins on his heels and leaves, Viola and Nyx trailing after him. There's perfect silence in the room. My head aches. For a second, I wish I was back in a coma.

I stare at the two alien Draekons who are supposedly my mates. What the fuck happens now?

Ryanna breaks the quiet with a chuckle. "Well," she says dryly. "I think it's safe to say that after that, Arax will be spending the night on the couch." She gets to her feet. "Come on, Sofia. We'll leave the lovers to it."

The two of them leave, and it's just the three of us. Dennox. Vulrux. And in the middle, me.

Great. Stupid orange goo that kills me. No chocolate. And now, this. Two alien mates.

I lift my chin up and give them a defiant glance. "Before you say anything," I say, my voice harsh. "Let's make one thing perfectly clear. I don't care how magical your dicks are. I'm not going to sleep with you."

5

Dennox:

I'd expected tears and pouting from the human woman when she heard the Firstborn's pronouncement. Instead, I get defiance.

Defiance is better. Much better. Defiance is *interesting*.

I've never felt the urge to throttle the Firstborn as much as I do at this moment. What does Arax think he's doing? We are not his puppets, to be mated at will.

Harper Boyd tilts her chin up and glares at Vulrux and me, her sea-blue eyes sparkling with anger. She's so tiny, this human woman who tugs at my dragon's heart.

She's also a complete stranger, and though we've been on this planet for a very long time, and I haven't known a woman's touch in sixty years, I've never bedded a woman who was unwilling, and I'm not about to start now.

She's yours, my dragon growls. *Take the woman. Claim her.*

"That's fine," I tell her calmly. I give Vulrux a questioning glance. "What now?"

He raises his shoulder in a shrug. "My cousin spends

much of his waking hours worrying about the women taken by the other exile batch," he says. "Especially after they almost took Viola. He's not thinking rationally. Let's give Viola a couple of days to work on him, and then he'll realize that he can't involve the human woman this way."

"Ahem." Harper Boyd speaks up. "Can you stop talking about me like I'm not here?"

Vulrux looks embarrassed. "My apologies, Harper Boyd. You've been in a coma, and we got into the habit of having conversations in this room." He gives our reluctant mate a searching look. "How are you feeling?" he asks her. "Is your arm numb? Any pain anywhere?"

She shakes her head. "I'm itching to get up," she says. "I'm feeling a little cooped up. What do you guys do for fun on this planet?"

That's a good question. The answer is that we don't have time for fun. There are fourteen of us on a hostile planet. Our energy goes toward surviving.

"It's the rainy season," I reply. "We mend our weapons so that we may hunt once the lowlands are dry again."

"Lovely," she says with a grimace. "So, I'm stuck here in this room?"

Her body is stronger now than it was when she first woke from her coma. The medicinal broths we've been feeding her have gone a long way to restoring her strength, but she's still frail. Rest is the best thing for her, but I can't bear the look of disappointment on her face. "There's somewhere I go when I want to be alone," I tell her. "If you want, we will take you there."

She starts to get up, and then her face turns red. "I need to get dressed."

Her body is naked under the sheet she's clutching, and I've heard from Nyx that the humans are strangely embarrassed by nudity. "Of course." I gesture to a small table. "Your clothes have been cleaned. Vulrux and I will leave you alone unless you need help?"

She shakes her head. "I can manage."

In five minutes, she's ready, dressed again in her off-world clothing. She looks pale and tired, and part of me wishes she'd stay in bed, but from the expression on her face, I can tell that she's determined to go exploring. I hand her a thin cloak, made from the leaves of the *watlich* tree. The cloak will not shield her fully from the rains, but it will provide some protection before it dissolves from the force of the deluge. "Come," I tell her.

"No need to tell the human where we're going," she murmurs under her breath. "Come, Harper. Go, Harper. Fetch, Harper. Roll over, Harper."

I frown in confusion at her words. What is she talking about? "Do you wish to come with us or not?"

She nods. "Don't mind me," she says. "My sarcasm switch is stuck in the 'On' position. Feel free to ignore everything I say."

She sways a little on her feet as she speaks. We're at her side immediately. "Perhaps you should rest," Vulrux says, looking concerned. "I don't want you over-exerting yourself."

She rolls her eyes at him. "I bet you anything that if I spread my legs, you'll be quite happy to let me over-exert myself."

That makes me laugh. Vulrux grins in amusement. "Fair enough, Harper Boyd," he says. "Fine. If you feel faint, lean on us for support."

She gives us a cautious look as if she doesn't quite understand us. That feeling goes both ways. "Harper Boyd sounds really formal," she says at last. "Call me Harper."

Harper:

Confession: I kinda want to spend more time with Vulrux and Dennox. There is something about these guys that makes me want to get to know them more. I tell myself that it's only natural for me to be interested in the two men that took care of me while I was ill, but I have a sneaking suspicion that I'm lying to myself. I can't stop staring at their bronze skin, their rippling muscles, and the tattoos that cover their bodies, and I'm completely fascinated by their nipple piercings.

Oh, who am I kidding? I'm attracted to them. It's super-annoying. I mean, newborn kittens are probably stronger than me. I'm still recovering from a coma, and I'm lusting after the first two guys I saw when I woke up?

C'mon, Harper. Stop drooling and pull yourself together. You're no Sleeping Beauty.

The two aliens—my so-called mates—guide me toward the door. They've got their arms around my waist, and they're practically holding me up. It'd actually be easier if one of them carried me.

Of course, if they tried it, I'd knee them in the groin.

Thinking about kneeing them in the groin makes my mind wander to dragon junk. Vulrux and Dennox are huge; Dennox, in particular, is built like a freight truck. I bet their cocks are proportional to their height. Judging from the way she simpered at Arax and Nyx earlier, Viola seems to have no complaints about their *equipment.*

Another, much dirtier thought strikes me. "When you transform into dragons," I ask them, trying to keep my voice casual, "how big do you become?"

Vulrux smirks at me. Hang on. He can't know I'm wondering what actual dragon dick looks like, can he? I decide he can't.

"I've only transformed once," he replies. He looks at Dennox. "How big did I get?"

"About the size of this room," Dennox replies. "Maybe a bit larger?"

Whoa. Hello, big boy.

Get your mind out of the gutter, Harper. Remember that speech you made, just two minutes ago? You are absolutely not going to sleep with gorgeous, sexy, outrageously ripped aliens.

Of course, the moment I make that declaration, my mind starts imagining it. *In vivid detail.* Can you blame me? There's two of them, and judging by the tightness of their pants, they're huge. And they're my own personal shirtless tour guides, eager to see to my every need.

Pinch me. I'm dreaming.

Shaking my head, I lean on Dennox as Vulrux opens the door. The instant I step outside, I stop dead in my tracks. I was bracing for a downpour, but nothing could have prepared me for this. This isn't rain. This is a solid wall of water.

Vulrux points to a covered passageway. "We're heading to the dining area," he says over the thunderous roar.

"How exciting," I say dryly. "Is there a feast? Has the tribe sacrificed a unicorn for my recovery?"

His eyes are amused. Evidently, these aliens can decipher sarcasm. *Oops.* "We're not going to eat," he says, his lips quirking up. My stomach does a funny little flip in response. Stupid stomach. "Unless you're hungry?"

Who knows what kind of weird food they have on this planet. Maybe they eat worms. *Blech.* "I'm fine," I say hastily. I'm transfixed by the sheer volume of water falling from the sky. I owe Viola an apology. She's right—no one can go in search of the other women in this weather.

Dennox mistakes my hesitation for fear. "I can carry you, Harper," he offers.

"Don't even think about it, buddy," I warn him. "Or I will break your arms."

"Is that so?" He laughs outright at me, and I grin back. Okay, I guess his amusement is totally warranted. Dennox is massive. Even at full strength, I'm not going to be able to hurt him. "Let's make a deal. If you stumble, I will pick you up."

You know what? Both Vulrux and Dennox are being pretty damn nice, especially considering my 'you don't have magic dicks; I'm not going to sleep with you' pronouncement. They haven't once brought up the whole 'I'm your mate' thing. I refuse to believe that I'm stuck on this planet forever, and I still have no intention of mating with them. But so far this morning, I've managed to piss off Viola, and I'm not sure where I stand with Sofia and Ryanna either. I could really use some friends.

We walk through the passageway. "How do the roofs stand up?" I marvel as we walk the short distance. I have to shout to make myself heard above the noise of the storm. "Doesn't the rain damage them?"

"We rebuild every year," Dennox replies.

Ouch. No wonder they don't have time for fun.

The dining hall is empty when we get there. It's a large space. There's an inner room, as well as a patio-like area, with a roof but no walls.

"Follow me," Vulrux says, leading the way into the inner room. In a corner, behind a counter, is a trap door.

Vulrux opens it, and I peer in. "There's a staircase," I say, astonished. "Where does it go?"

"It's Dennox's pet project," Vulrux replies. "I'll let him tell you."

I turn to Dennox with a raised eyebrow, but he shakes his head. "You'll find out."

Okay, buddy. Be mysterious.

We walk down a flight of wooden stairs which seem to go on forever. Finally, we get to the bottom. I follow Vulrux through a stone archway and realize that we've reached a vast underground lake.

My mouth falls open. We've found Paradise. There are a couple of naturally occurring skylights in the ceiling, through which rain falls in a steady downpour. Most of the lake is sheltered though, and the water is a clear, inviting shade of turquoise. "How did you find this place?" I ask Dennox, astonished. "It's absolutely gorgeous. Did you build the stairs? How did you tunnel into the mountain?"

"It is beautiful," Dennox agrees, his lips twitching at my flood of questions. "I found it by accident." He points to one of the skylights. "I fell through," he says ruefully. "There are many natural tunnels inside the mountain. Once I knew where the lake was, it was a relatively simple matter to find a tunnel that led to the peak. I didn't have to do a lot of digging."

Vulrux snorts. "Not a lot of digging? It took five years to build the stairs."

Dennox seems uncomfortable with the praise. He moves toward the water, giving me a look over his shoulder. "Nyx told me that many people in your world swim. Do you not know how?"

I snort. I almost made the national team. I taught swimming in high school back home. "Yes, of course I know how to swim."

Dennox drops his pants and turns around to give me a questioning look. "What are you waiting for?"

My throat goes dry. All my questions about dragon junk have been answered. This isn't the first cock I've seen in my life, but it's the first alien cock, *and it is fine.*

Dennox wades into the water. Vulrux gets naked as well and climbs onto a nearby cluster of rocks. I shamelessly check out his tight, sculpted ass, and my insides clench hard. I owe Viola an apology. If her naked guys are anywhere as hot as mine, I fully understand why she's uninterested in getting rescued.

Vulrux gets to the top and prepares to dive. "What's the matter, Harper?" he asks. "Are you feeling too tired to jump in?"

"No," I mutter, my face heating. They're so casual about their nudity, and I'm being a prude, but NASA's finest astrogear was not made for immersion in water. "I don't have a swimsuit."

Vulrux looks confused. "You have a lovely body," he says. "Why do you want to cover it?"

Dennox splashes some water in my direction. "I assure you," he says, his solemn tone a contrast to the playful gesture, "that we will not claim you without your consent. It is not our way."

It's not them I'm worried about. It's me. If I'm naked in the water with them, I'm not sure I can keep myself from doing some *accidental* groping.

Vulrux's lips twitch at my indecision. He doesn't try to persuade me again. He dives into the water, his body cleanly slicing through the surface of the lake, and emerges, shaking water from his hair. The light catches his nipple rings. I never thought I was a piercing sort of girl, but damn. I just want to take them in my teeth and—

Stop it, Harper.

The guys splash around while I linger on the shore. Damn them. This is a hot, humid planet. My clothing sticks uncomfortably to my body, and a dip in the lake sounds wonderful. The water is clear and blue and calling to me.

I watch them longingly for a few minutes. Dennox and Vulrux aren't looking in my direction. They're talking with each other, and not paying any attention to me, a fact that should make me happy but instead fills me with unexpected pique. *They won't even notice if you get naked, Harper,* I think sourly. *You're denying yourself for no reason.*

Fuck it. I strip off my clothes and jump into the water, sighing in pleasure at the blissful coolness. I haven't stepped in a pool for almost a year. After Tom, my spiteful and mean-spirited ex-boyfriend had forced me to quit my high-school swim coach job, I'd lost the desire to swim. Now, on an alien planet, my love for the water comes rushing back.

I strike out in the direction of some glowing blue bushes, then remember my encounter with the orange fungus. I've had my fair share of murderous plants. I swim toward Dennox and Vulrux. "Is there anything poisonous here?"

Vulrux shakes his head. "You're safe." He looks at my right palm and his expression changes to one of concern. "Bast," he swears. "You're bleeding again."

I look at my hand. Sure enough, my cut, which had knit together, has opened. "It doesn't hurt," I assure them. A scary thought strikes me. "It's not going to attract blood sucking leeches, is it?"

"What are blood sucking leeches?" Dennox asks. "I do not understand what the translator is saying."

I try and explain a leech to the aliens. They nod as if they understand, but I'm not sure if I've managed to communicate the concept. "Speaking of blood," I say, changing the topic, "A few days ago, the two of you were holding my hand, and you were both bleeding as well. Were you giving me some kind of transfusion?"

Vulrux and Dennox glance at each other. Dennox grimaces, rubbing the tattoos on his arms. "Yes," Vulrux says, after a moment of silence. "According to Raiht'vi, the Draekons have immunity to the *enrak*. When our blood mingled, we passed that on to you."

That seems reasonable. I don't understand why the two men look so wary. "Why are you looking like I'm going to freak out?"

Dennox clears his throat. It's a very human gesture, and it strikes me how weird it is that I feel so comfortable with them. Will Smith would have shot the aliens. I'm fantasizing about jumping them.

"The Draekon mutation is now in your bloodstream, Harper Boyd. We had to do it to save your life, but there's a catch."

I'm not an idiot. I can connect the dots. "I got immunity to the orange goop," I whisper. "What else did I get from your blood?"

"I don't know," Vulrux replies frankly. "As a result of the mating bond, Viola Lewis has become stronger, faster. You might react the same way, or it might be something else. The mutation always has an effect."

Both of them are bracing themselves for my reaction. I should be upset, I guess, but I can't summon up much anger. Yeah, even as I swim, the Draekon mutation is in my veins, doing God-knows-what to my insides. Then again, had the two men not acted, I would have died. The primary emotion I'm feeling is gratitude. "You saved my life," I say softly. "I'm here. I'm alive, and I'm swimming. Viola seems unharmed by the mutation. I'm not going to worry about possible side effects right now." I take a deep breath. "I'm just going to enjoy the lake. Thank you for bringing me here."

That's when I see a movement in the water.

A ten-foot long crimson-red water snake is swimming toward the three of us.

I shriek like a little girl.

Just when I started to think things weren't too bad after all...

Orange goo, non-stop rain, humidity that makes my hair frizz, and now a massive red snake in the water?

Fuck this shit. The prison planet is doing its level best to kill me. I need to get the hell away from here.

6

Vulrux:

A red *narmi* swims lazily toward Harper. The moment her eyes fall on it, she screams and grabs me by the waist. "What is that thing?" she squeals, positioning herself between Dennox and me.

Her soft breasts press against my back, and my cock hardens with lust. She smells like fresh air and sunlight, and I want her with a sudden, fiery need. From Dennox's strangled groan, he is overtaken by the same heady lust.

It is tempting to stay where I am and enjoy the way she feels. It's been a long time since I've had a woman touch me so intimately. Her hands are tight around my waist, and if she moves them just a little lower, she'll graze my cock.

And yet, I cannot. Harper Boyd is still recovering from her brush with the orange *enrak*. Right now, she is dangerously out of balance. Everything on this planet feels like a threat to her.

Including us.

I would bed her gladly but now is not the time.

Dennox must feel the same way I do because he disengages himself from Harper's grasp. "The *narmi* are friendly." He whistles to the red snake as it swims past us, and it turns when it hears the sound and approaches us, butting Dennox's palm affectionately. "The red ones are very intelligent," he continues, stroking the *narmi*. "And harmless. This one just wants some berries."

"Holy crap," Harper whispers. "You guys have a pet snake. A pet water snake."

I don't know anything about the planet that Harper Boyd comes from. "Do you not have pets on Earth?"

"We do." She gulps. "I'm not so sure about snakes in the water. Some people swim with dolphins, and I've always wanted to do that. It's on my bucket list, but it's an expensive trip. But this," she shudders, "seems a lot closer to getting in a tank and being dropped into shark-infested waters."

Dennox and I give her blank looks, and she laughs sheepishly. "I babble when I'm nervous," she mumbles. "The snake freaked me out." She puts her hand out and pats the *narmi* on the head tentatively. "Hey buddy," she croons. "You're not planning on wrapping your body around me and squeezing, are you? No cobra-like moves from you. That's a good boy."

Harper:

Muscles. Lots and lots of yummy, *yummy* muscles.

Yes, I grabbed onto Dennox and Vulrux by sheer instinct, freaked out by the appearance of the long red snake in the water.

But after that?

Did I hold on to them for just a little longer, even though I was in no danger?

Yes, I did.

Did I grind my ass into Dennox's cock?

Yes, I did.

Did I ache to move my fingers lower and brush against Vulrux's hard-on?

Guilty as charged.

Am I wet right now, turned on by the idea of their hard dicks sliding into me?

Yes, I am.

You know what the worst thing is? The absolute worst thing is that both men can tell the way I'm feeling. They're not blind. They can see the way my nipples have pebbled and hardened. There's a smirk on Vulrux's lips and a glimmer of amusement in Dennox's eyes.

"I'm still not going to sleep with you," I murmur, my cheeks flaming, afraid to meet their eyes. "Even if your dicks are magical."

Vulrux stifles a laugh. "Of course," he says blandly. "Unless you want to swim some more, we should head back."

I seize on that suggestion. Yes. It's so much safer in the camp. Vulrux and Dennox will be clothed. There will be other people around, Draekon and human. In camp, I'll be able to resist the two men.

I think.

MY SWIM HAS LEFT me more tired than I'm prepared to admit. "Rest," Vulrux orders me when we're back in what I think of as my bedroom. "If you over-exert yourself, you'll suffer a relapse."

"Who made you the boss of me?" I retort sullenly.

Dennox raises an eyebrow. "If you don't do as you're told," he says calmly, "I will tie you to the bed myself."

Damn it. My brain immediately goes into overdrive. The pictures flicker through my head. I'm tied to the bed, legs and arms spread wide, naked except for a thin sheet over me. Vulrux and Dennox stand on either side of the bed. One of them rips the sheet off me, and their eyes heat with lust. I can't close my legs, and I can't squirm away from them. *Not that I want to.* They'll run their hands down my body, exploring every inch of me, watching as I writhe and moan in response.

Harper Boyd, stop this nonsense right now.

Dennox's nostrils flare. "I can smell your arousal," he says silkily. "I don't understand your human ways, Harper Boyd. You want us. Your mind is picturing our mating even now, isn't it? Why do you deny yourself?"

Because I feel powerless in this world. I feel fragile and out-of-control, and I don't like it.

If I sleep with the irresistible dragons, it'll be to avoid reality. To pretend, for the space of a few stolen moments, that I'm not stuck on an alien planet.

The sex will probably be very good, but it'll only complicate an already fucked-up situation.

"I'm going to take a nap."

Of course, the Draekons know I'm avoiding answering Dennox's question, but thankfully, they don't push me.

I SLEEP FOR A FEW HOURS. When I wake, the sun is low in the sky, and I'm starving. "I'm sure you can find food, Harper," I say out loud. "They probably don't eat maggots. This isn't Survivor."

I get dressed in NASA's finest astro-gear, wishing for a change of clothing. Vulrux and Dennox can probably find me something that'll work as a needle. Maybe I can MacGyver myself a dress from their towels. Anything has to be better than government-issued Spandex. It's supposed to wick away moisture, but as we discovered the first time we ventured out into the jungle, it's no match for the humidity on this planet.

Neither Vulrux nor Dennox appears to be around. I don't wait for them; I grab the cloak Dennox gave me and head out toward the dining room.

Earlier today, I was too busy marveling at the deluge of rain to notice the design of the passageways. Now, I realize that several houses are dotted around the clearing, and each of them has a covered passage connecting it to the dining hall. Clever.

Viola said that there were fourteen Draekon, and they've been exiled for sixty years. My mind struggles to comprehend those numbers. I live in California. I'm always surrounded by people. Driving to work in the mornings, I used to mutter curses about gridlock. Now, my entire world has shrunk to fourteen Draekon and three human women.

Stay strong. I hear my mother's voice in my head. She was my swim coach. I would whine about my muscles hurting, and my mother wouldn't relent. *Nothing worthwhile comes easy, little dolphin,* she would tell me. *Stay strong and focus on what's important.*

What's important now? Not sex with hot dragons. No, my focus should be finding a way to rescue Olivia, May, and the others, and getting the fuck off this planet.

Speaking of the other women, I need to apologize to Viola. I was a bitch earlier, and I shouldn't have yelled at her. I have no right to judge her choices. If she wants to stay on this planet, that's her call.

The dining hall is almost empty. I'm either too early for dinner or too late. Given how loudly my stomach is rumbling, I hope it's the latter.

There's only one Draekon there. Thankfully for me, it's the one who was guarding me earlier. He's throwing knives at something that looks like a dart board. He turns when he hears me approach, and a friendly smile breaks out on his face when he recognizes me. "Are you hungry, Harper Boyd? I'm preparing the night meal now, but if you'd like, I can find you something to eat while you wait."

Somehow, I doubt there's a refrigerator filled with snacks.

"Do you all eat together?" I ask curiously. The dining hall is large enough, and it's dominated by one long table and more than a dozen chairs.

He nods. "During the dry season, the fourteen of us traverse the lowlands, and we don't get many opportunities to share meals. During the rainy season, however, it is customary to eat the evening meal together."

That actually sounds nice. When I was dating Tom, one of the best things about the relationship was that I had someone to cook for, someone to eat dinner with. Even if Tom's eyes were always glued to the TV screen, and he never once thanked me for the meal.

Then again, Tom was always a jerk. I should have listened to my friends when they tried to warn me.

"I'm looking for Viola. Do you know which house she's in?"

He points to a house in the distance, one with a porch wrapped all around the outside. I can almost imagine sitting there in a rocking chair, watching the rain fall. "The Firstborn and Viola Lewis live in Nyx's house," he says. "If you are looking for Sofia Menendez or Ryanna, they are in the Firstborn's quarters." He points to a surprisingly small and unassuming house not too far from us.

Once I'm done talking to Viola, I need to have a conversation with Raiht'vi. If the Draekon mutation is working its sinister magic on me, I'd like to know what to expect. The tall Zorahn scientist doesn't strike me as particularly forthcoming, but she did tell Dennox and Vulrux how to cure me. Maybe she's friendlier than I think. "What about the two scientists," I ask Thrax. "Where can I find them?"

His body tenses. "Beirax and Raiht'vi are recovering in Zorux's house," he says, pointing to a walkway on his left. "That way."

"Good to know," I tell him cheerfully. "Thank you."

His lips tighten. "I would avoid the scientists if I were you, Harper Boyd," he says. "When Beirax is healthy, he will stand trial for his crimes. As for the Highborn Scientist? Vulrux does not trust her, and neither does Dennox. In sixty years, I've learned that neither men are hasty to form judgments. You would do well to heed their caution."

Viola might be sweet and pliable, and she might do everything Arax and Nyx tell her. The sooner the rest of the Draekon learn that all Earth women aren't quite as compliant, the better. I pat Thrax on the arm. "Dennox and Vulrux aren't the bosses of me."

7

Dennox:

Harper looks exhausted. As soon as she announces her desire to sleep, Vulrux and I leave her alone so she may rest.

The moment the two of us head outside, I place my hand on the healer's arm. "I need to talk to you."

Vulrux looks both surprised and wary. "Of course," he says. We head to the dining room, but Thrax and Zorux are there, preparing the evening meal. "Let's go to your house," he suggests.

Perhaps he can sense that I need privacy for what I'm going to say. I lead the way to my simple one-room dwelling. Zoraken are trained to be hardy, and even after sixty years, the ways that were beaten into me are hard to let go.

Once we're inside, I turn to my pair-bond. "We've never talked about the Crimson Citadel," I begin.

"What's there to say?" Vulrux asks bitterly, staring out of the small front window. "We couldn't protect our mate."

It haunts me too. That woman died because the two of

us transformed to Draekon when we set eyes on her. We're responsible.

I've relived that night a million times. It's quite ironic. My memory is fragmented as a result of the Zoraken mind-wipes. I can't remember the faces of my parents. I can't remember the wars I've fought in. But the look on the face of the woman whose name I never knew, as the guards turned their weapons toward her? *That, I can't forget.*

"I don't want to talk about her death," I reply flatly. It's the gaps in my memory that I want to discuss with Vulrux. "Have you heard about the Zoraken mind-wipes?"

Vulrux looks intrigued. "I've heard rumors. So it's true?"

I nod. No one ever talks about what it takes to become a soldier of the Empire, but the costs are high. Our memories are wiped when we are first recruited, so that we will devote all our energy to training, sparing no thought for our families. They're wiped after battle, so we can ignore the emotional trauma that comes with war.

The first wipe is hard; the mind wants to cling to its memories. The subsequent ones are easier, but each time we are tampered with, we become unstable. I've been wiped eighteen times, a statistic that's carved on my skin with blunt knife strokes, one slash for each time I went under. The record is twenty-one. No Zoraken in the history of the High Empire has survived their twenty-second wipe.

"Yes." My voice is clipped. I don't like talking about the past, but I need Vulrux's help. "I can only remember fragments."

I draw a deep breath and share one of my deepest fears. "I don't remember how I ended up in the Crimson Citadel," I blurt out. "I was at the Battle of Adrash, but after that, I can't remember anything. For the Zoraken to give me to the scientists as a prisoner, I must have done something terrible..." My pulse races and my skin grows cold and clammy. For sixty years, I've had recurring nightmares about the battlefield. I've had nightmares in which I've watched children die, nightmares in which I didn't do anything to prevent the carnage. "What if I'm a monster, Vulrux?"

He shakes his head. "I don't know why you were in that underground lab. Only the scientists know that. But," he adds, his voice calm and quiet, "I know you, Dennox. You've been my friend for sixty years. You are not a monster. You are a good man."

"Am I? I'm a soldier, Vulrux. My soul is stained and tattered."

"You were sent into battle by the High Emperor Dravex," he retorts. "You obeyed orders and did your duty. My uncle will be tested in the Gardens of Caeron, not you."

I'm not reassured. "I thought I could live with not knowing what lay in my past," I say harshly. "But things have changed now. Harper is our mate, but until I know the truth about why I was imprisoned at the citadel, I won't touch her."

Vulrux stares at me. "You are Draekon," he says after a long pause. "Your dragon will not allow you to resist her."

"It doesn't matter." In the dining room, Thrax must have finished preparing the meal, because he's now throwing bone knives at a target on the wall, practicing the smooth strokes that help us bring down the *argangana*. "The only thing I have left is my honor. If I am capable of hurting Harper, then it does not matter what the dragon inside me wants. I will fall on my sword before I take that risk."

My words are a lie. Already, I'm finding it difficult to resist the tug I feel toward her. Already, I've been telling myself that I won't be able to hurt my mate... I'm making excuses because I'm attracted to the golden-haired human woman.

"Is that what you wanted to tell me?" Vulrux asks harshly. "That you plan on killing yourself?" He draws himself up to his full height, and when he speaks, he speaks with the authority of the Highborn. "I, Vulrux, Thirdborn of Zoraht, forbid it. There will be no more death."

"I didn't bring you here to ask for permission, *Highborn*. I was hoping that you might be able to find a way to bring back the memories. Perhaps an herb? A potion? This planet teems with medicinal plants. Is there something here that could recover my missing years?"

"Ah." Vulrux realizes he jumped to conclusions, and to his credit, looks sheepish. "Forgive me."

His apology is unexpected. Vulrux is the Thirdborn of Zoraht. Only three people in the High Empire were more powerful than he was, the High Emperor Dravex, Arax, and Lenox, yet both Arax and Vulrux can admit when they are in the wrong.

"I can't think of any plant that improves the memory," he continues. "But there is still hope, Dennox. There is always hope. On her world, Viola Lewis devoted herself to the study of plants. Sofia Menendez is a healer. We can use their help. *We will find a way to bring your memories back.*"

A thin tendril of hope coils around my heart. On the prison planet, I've found the freedom I never had as one of the Zoraken. I don't need to kill. I don't need to wage war in the name of the High Emperor.

Underneath the hope though, is a deep well of unease.

The truth will either set me free, or it will trap me forever.

～

Harper:

I find Viola alone. "Where are your pet dragons?" I ask her. Then my brain catches up with my mouth, and I realize that that might not be the most diplomatic of openings. "Sorry. I meant Arax and Nyx."

She chuckles. "I quite like the sound of pet dragons," she says. "Come on in. You have no idea how good it is to see you up and about. You want something to drink?"

I stare at her. "There are drinks on this planet?"

She rolls her eyes. "Harper," she says patiently. "On Earth, humans have been making beer for over seven thousand years. The Zorahn and the Draekon are alien races, but they're not that different from us. Yes, they have drinks. Want some *kunnr* wine? It tastes like a thin vanilla milkshake, but packs one hell of a punch."

"Sure." I sit down on a long wooden bench. "Umm, I'm sorry I yelled at you earlier."

Viola hands me a red wooden cup. "No worries," she says easily. "You'd just woken up from a coma, and we threw a lot of information at you. We told you that you were stuck on this planet, and then you found out you have two mates. I'd probably have reacted the same way."

I take an experimental sip of the beverage. Viola's described it perfectly. It tastes like a very smooth, very alcoholic milkshake, and it is delicious. I've got to see if Dennox and Vulrux can rustle me up some of this stuff.

"Would you?" I ask her. "You seem happy here, Vi. You're coping much better than I am." My lips twist. "I can't seem to get past 'I'm stuck on an alien planet with no hope of rescue.'"

"I'm being practical, Harper. I'm living in the present, and enjoying what I have." She gazes into her drink. "My father died of leukemia," she says quietly. "I spent most of his illness in denial. I read research papers. I talked to doctors, hoping he could qualify for experimental cures. If I could go back, you know what I would do instead?" She looks sad. "I'd hug my father. I'd talk to him and do jigsaw puzzles with him, drink whiskey with him and tell him that I love him."

She takes a deep breath. I pretend not to notice the tears in her eyes. "Arax and Nyx love me," she says. "And I love them. If I start thinking about the possibility of getting rescued, I will once again fail to enjoy what I have. Right now, I'm safe. I'm secure, and I'm loved. It's better than what I had back on Earth."

The mood in the room has turned serious. Time for some levity, Harper Boyd-style. "If Arax and Nyx are as well endowed as Vulrux and Dennox," I quip, grinning widely at her, "you're *very* well-loved."

Her eyes go wide, and she chokes on her cup of wine. "You slept with them?" she asks when she stops coughing. "When did this happen?"

"That came out wrong," I say hastily, my cheeks flushing. "Of course I didn't sleep with them. They took me swimming, and they didn't have swim trunks, so I caught a glimpse of their, umm, equipment."

"Oh." She eyes me curiously. "Did you have fun?"

I know what Viola's hinting at. Rather than beat around the bush, I get right to the point. "I like having choices, Vi. I don't like other people planning my life for me. Yeah, Vulrux and Dennox are nice. Back on Earth, I'd have gone out with them if they'd asked me on a date. But here, they're my mates, and we're supposed to spend time together so that we can complete the mating bond, *and I don't even know what the mating bond is.*" My lips tighten with frustration. "Pardon me for not being ecstatic about the situation."

"I don't think anyone really understands the mating bond," she replies. "Here's what I know. When two Draekons find their mate, they transform into dragons. But the transformation is only half-complete at that stage, and the Draekons cannot change at will. For that to happen, the trio needs to consummate the relationship."

"So Vulrux and Dennox turned into dragons when they saw me?" I ask Viola. "Is that how everyone's so certain they're my mates?"

"Not exactly," she says. "They had a mate in the past, but she was killed before the bond could be completed."

"What?" I gape at the brown-haired botanist. "Killed? How? Why?"

She looks uncomfortable. "I don't know if I should tell you the details," she murmurs. "I don't think Vulrux and Dennox like talking about it, and I don't want to gossip."

"Viola, this isn't idle gossip. We're talking about my life here."

"Fair enough," she admits. She tells me the story, and I listen, transfixed. When she's done, my emotions are in turmoil. I've been pouting all day because I'm trapped on this planet, but as I'm beginning to realize, everyone here is a captive, and everyone has a story of heartbreak. Poor Dennox and Vulrux. "When you showed up, they knew you were their mate," Viola concludes. "You're their second chance."

"Ah." Understanding and a deep unease fills me. "Arax is expecting trouble with the other exile batch, isn't he? That's why he wants Vulrux and Dennox to be able to transform freely."

"I think he's preparing for the worst-case scenario," she replies.

This situation sucks. If the five women are being held prisoner, then I want to do whatever it takes to rescue them. *Except it means that I'm going to have to sleep with the two men.* "So I'm to be the sacrificial lamb," I say, my tone tinged with bitterness. "That's why I'm being forced to spend time with Dennox and Vulrux."

Come on, Harper. You enjoy Dennox and Vulrux's company. Why are you acting like they are horrible people?

Viola seems to understand my conflicting emotions. "I'll talk to Arax," she says. "Harper, I promise you. Nobody's going to make you do anything you don't want. We'll find a way to rescue the other women, with or without Vulrux and Dennox transforming. Besides," she adds, "Ryanna and Sofia might find Draekon mates. Ryanna likes Thrax."

"And Sofia?"

To my surprise, she doesn't respond right away. "To be honest," she says after a long pause, "I thought Sofia and Vulrux had a thing going."

I'm shocked by the surge of jealousy that runs through my body. "Why?"

"They're both doctors," she replies. "They've spent a lot of time together. Mostly focused on treating you," she adds hastily. She shrugs. "The Draekons have been celibate for a very long time," she adds. "I thought that maybe the two of them would hook up, that's all."

"Won't that trigger this magic mating bond?"

"I think the magic mating bond needs a threesome," she quips. "Regular, old-fashioned, non-kinky, one-on-one sex is still allowed, as far as I know."

The thought of Vulrux and Sofia having sex makes me feel sick. I don't like it. Not one little bit. Since the moment I woke up, everyone's been talking about Vulrux and Dennox as if they're mine, and evidently, my subconscious agrees.

Don't be a bitch, Harper, my conscience prods me again. *You keep saying you don't want to have sex with Vulrux and Dennox, yet the moment someone else might be interested, you're possessive about them?*

Damn it.

"Oh, I almost forgot," Viola says, jumping to her feet. "I've a surprise for you."

"I think today's quota of surprises has been reached already."

She grins at me. "Trust me, you're going to like this one." She hurries from the room and reappears a moment later with a navy-blue suitcase. "Ta-dah," she says.

I stare at it. "Is that my luggage?"

"Yup." She beams widely. "Arax and Nyx went to get everyone's luggage before the rains hit. They cleaned the spaceship out pretty good."

A sudden thought occurs to me. "Was there a working communication system?" I ask her. "Can we talk to the other Zorahn? Or to someone on Earth?"

She looks somber. "I already asked. It was broken."

My head is spinning, a combination of the *kunnr* wine and the after-effects of the orange fungus. I want to try and figure out an escape plan, but right now, some food and another nap sound infinitely more tempting. Just then, a loud, shrill horn blast cuts through the air.

"Dinner," Viola says. "There'll be a full house tonight. Everyone knows you're awake, and word has got around that Vulrux and Dennox claimed you as their mate. Prepare for some curious looks."

My stomach rumbles loudly. "The aliens can gawk all they want," I tell Viola. "As long as they feed me first."

8

Vulrux:

After my disquieting talk with Dennox, I head to Zorux's house to check on the two scientists, carrying a tray of food in my hands. Both scientists have declined to eat with the Draekons, choosing instead to be served in their rooms. They're still weak from their wounds, and so we tolerate it.

As I walk down the long passageway to the western-most edge of the clearing, I'm lost in thought. If there is an herb that will bring back my pair-bond's missing memories, I've never heard of it.

On the homeworld, mind-wipes are administered by the Technicians. It is rumored that they also possess the ability to undo them. Unfortunately, here on the prison planet, technicians are in short supply, as is the equipment they need to do their job.

If only I had finished my training before the exile...

I understand only too well Dennox's ache for the truth. My own such need is what drives me to Zorux's house, with a small bottle of *ahuma* venom concealed in my robes.

Both Raiht'vi and Beirax are well enough to be questioned. Arax had a short, unproductive conversation with the male scientist a few days ago, but the meeting had ended in an impasse. Arax wants Beirax banished as a result of his crimes. Beirax tried to exchange information for a pardon, but my cousin was not in a forgiving mood.

Raiht'vi's injuries are almost healed, and she wears the white robes, a rare honor among the scientists, one reserved for only their best and brightest. If anyone knows the truth of who ordered my mate to be killed in the Crimson Citadel, it would be her.

Yet when I reach the entrance to the room in which she is recuperating, I hesitate. Without Raiht'vi's help, Harper would have died. I don't want to feel any sense of obligation to the scientist, but I do.

Beirax then.

I enter the scientist's room. He's awake, staring out of the window at the rains with a bleak expression on his face. "Does it ever stop?" he asks, his voice tight with frustration. "How do you stand it?"

"You get used to it," I reply.

I don't know what I think of the scientist. Beirax's actions have led to the death of two people, the technician Mannix and the human woman Janet, but had he not crashed the Zorahn spaceship on the prison planet, we would have never met Harper. To say I'm conflicted is an understatement.

Viola Lewis told us what Beirax said before he crashed the spaceship on the prison planet. If I understand correctly, he's trying to bring the Draekons to power, but I can't figure out why. The mysterious Order of the Crimson Night, the shadowy splinter group that Beirax belongs to, cannot possibly hope to benefit from Draekon rule. Even though it was a long-ago Zorahn Emperor, Kannix, that ordered the Draekon race into exile, it is the scientists who test us, and it is their gold-tipped needles that determine our fate. The Crimson Citadel has nothing to gain from Draekon ascendance.

Wheels within wheels. Secrets carefully guarded; knowledge hoarded. That is the Zorahn way. For sixty years, I've lived without the rigid rules that governed my home-world. Now, I feel myself drawn into the sticky web again.

Beirax is still looking out of the window. I set the tray down on a narrow table, and empty the bottle of *ahuma* venom into a steaming bowl of *argangana* broth. What I'm about to do violates every tenet of the healer code, but I don't care.

I need answers, and I intend to get them.

"How is the pain today?" Beirax was badly wounded in the crash. Sofia Menendez tells me that if he were human, he would have died of his wounds. Zorahn are sturdier. By the time the rains stop, Beirax will be back to full health.

"Manageable."

I hold my breath as he sits down at the table and drinks the entire bowlful of broth. The venom acts swiftly. In a minute, Beirax's breathing evens, and his eyes glaze. He's ready for the interrogation.

"Lie down on the bed," I instruct. I've had very limited opportunities to test the effects of the *ahuma* potion, and I'm unsure how long the effects will last, and how much infor-mation I'll be able to coax out of the scientist, particularly if he's taken safeguards against mind probes.

Beirax heads obediently to the cot and lies down.

My heart is pounding in my chest. For sixty years, I've

been dreaming about the moment when I find out the truth. Who ordered the guards to kill our mate? Now, the information is finally within my reach.

"In the Crimson Citadel, there are laboratories in the lower levels. Tell me what happens there."

"I don't know," Beirax replies instantly. "Only the most talented scientists work at those levels. Or so they say."

Frustration fills me. Beirax knows nothing.

Unless... The venom compels Beirax to answer my questions, but it won't make him volunteer information. I need to approach this matter from a different angle. I need answers, for Dennox's sake, and for mine.

"Fine. Tell me everything you've heard about the underground levels."

His forehead beads with sweat as he struggles to avoid answering. "I've heard it said," he says at last, "that in the caverns of the Citadel, we work on the Forbidden."

I frown in confusion. "What is the Forbidden?"

He answers that question readily. "After the Draekon rebellion," he says, "Kannix, Light of the Galaxies decreed that the scientists were forbidden from manipulating the threads of life. We were no longer permitted to create new races, and we were ordered to destroy our work on the Draekons."

I draw in a harsh breath. Every member of our society lives by one code. The word of the High Emperor is law. For the scientists to defy Kannix's order is treason. Treason punishable by death.

Beirax's words match up with my own observations. Dennox was being held prisoner in the Crimson Citadel, as was our mate. For generations, by order of the High Emperor, every person with the Draekon mutation is to be exiled to the prison planet, but it seems that the scientists diverted a few Draekons to their underground labs to experiment on them.

How high does the rot go? "Do the Council of Scientists know about the underground labs? Does Brunox know?"

He laughs shortly. "You're a naive fool, Thirdborn. Of course Brunox knows. A grain of sand could not stir in the Citadel without the Head of the Council finding out."

Outrage fills me. I bear no love for my cousin Lenox, but he needs to know about the treachery in his ranks. But how? There are no communicators here. When the Draekons are sent to the prison planet, it is a death sentence. I have no way of warning the High Emperor.

"Sixty years ago, a woman was killed in the underground labs. She was being held prisoner while your precious scientists experimented on her. Tell me what you know about her death."

"A Zorahn woman?"

I nod, and he shakes his head at once. "We don't experiment on our own kind. Our code forbids it."

"Or you aren't talented enough to run those experiments," I retort acidly.

His eyes flash with anger, and I regret my outburst. Antagonizing Beirax serves no purpose. From his own confession, he's a low-level underling who knows nothing.

Whether or not I feel gratitude toward Raiht'vi, I'm going to have to turn to her for information.

Beirax is still under the effects of the *ahuma* venom. "Who are the Order of the Crimson Night? What do you hope to achieve?"

Once again, Beirax strains to keep silent, but the venom is more potent than any truth serum found on the homeworld. "The conditions are right for the Draekons to return, but the Council is cautious and moves too slowly." His hands curl into fists as he tries to resist telling me what he knows. "The Order of the Crimson Night will bring the Draekons back within two generations. We will overturn the crystal throne. Scientists will finally rule over the High Empire."

I'm not sure if Beirax is talking about a credible plot to overthrow the High Empire, or if I'm listening to the ravings of a madman. "Why are the conditions right for the Draekons to return?"

"The mutation has spread," he replies. "At the last testing, two thousand Draekons were found. There are now enough males for our plan to take effect."

Two thousand! I stiffen with shock. Our exile batch had fourteen.

"Tell me about your plan."

Beirax's knuckles turn white as he tries to fight back. "I don't know it all," he replies. "I'm one of many. I was asked to find out if the human women could mate with the Draekons."

"And then what? This is a prison planet. Even if the human women produce Draekon young, we can't leave the planet. Your spaceship crashed. The communicator on it is broken. You're stuck here, as much as any of us. Your plan doesn't make any sense."

He sneers at me. "Once again, you take me for a fool, Thirdborn."

A prickle of unease runs down my spine. "Explain," I order.

"Every trap can be sprung," he replies. "There's a way out of this planet. For months, the Order of the Crimson Night has been dropping supplies on the prison planet. Somewhere out there," he says bitterly, waving his arm toward the window, "are the component parts of a Cloakship."

I inhale sharply. "That's impossible," I say harshly. "You cannot drop supplies on this planet. The Zorahn Navy patrols the skies above us, watching for any attempts to help the Exiles."

His smile doesn't reach his eyes. "And yet," he says, "The Zorahn Navy has turned a blind eye to our supply drops. Ask yourself, Thirdborn. If the Navy was keeping such a close watch on the prison planet, why did they not blast our spaceship to smithereens? Why did they let it land?"

He's being oblique. The effects of the potion are wearing away. I only have time for a few more questions and must focus on the most important matters. I have only one more vial of *ahuma* venom, and I must save that for questioning Raiht'vi.

I have to choose. I can either satisfy my curiosity about why the Zorahn Navy let *Fehrat 1* through, or I can question Beirax about the supply drops.

"You didn't land though, did you? You crashed."

"Raiht'vi interfered," he snaps. "Do you think this was supposed to be a suicide mission? I'd planned on landing near the drop site. I had a locator that would take me to the supplies. Mannix was a technician, and he would have assembled the Cloakship. The Draekon have sharper, faster reflexes. They would have piloted the ship through the asteroid belt. We'd thought of everything."

His expression turns bitter. "Raiht'vi ruined the plan. She locked me out of the controls. Because of her, we crashed nowhere near the planned location. The locator that will lead me to the cloakship is on *Fehrat 1,* submerged under water. Even if I could retrieve it, the supply drop zone is a two-month journey on foot, dangerously close to another exile batch." His voice is bleak. "I have no weapons, and I can't make my way across the jungle unarmed. It's too dangerous. I'm a scientist, not a warrior."

No. He's right. Beirax wouldn't last two days in the wild before the Dwals will catch his scent and hunt him.

"If one of the Exiles finds the Cloakship before I do..." His voice trails off. His lips tighten, and he glares at me mutinously.

He's resisting my questioning. I've run out of time. Time for the *ahuma's* last trick. "Sleep now. I order you to forget this conversation. When you wake, you will remember nothing."

His eyes shut. Within minutes, he's fast asleep.

This conversation has changed everything. There's a way off the prison planet. As soon as the rains stop, we need to find the locator, and let it guide us to the Cloakship.

Hope surges in my breast then recedes swiftly. If leaving the prison planet is possible, Harper's not going to want to stay.

Don't tell her just yet, a voice inside me urges. *Don't get her hopes up.*

I want to believe that I'm listening to that voice because I want to spare Harper's feelings, but that's not the real reason. The truth is that if I tell her, Dennox and I will lose our mate. Once again.

9

Harper:

Viola and I head to the dining hall, wheeling my suitcase behind me. It's darker now, and there are no lights, of course. "What do you do after dark?" I ask her as we walk. "And please don't say 'sex.' I mean, what do you do for light?"

"We have oil lamps," she replies. "Well, not oil. Tallow." She wrinkles her nose. "It can smell a bit fishy."

"So not everything is perfect?" I tease her.

She laughs. "I never said it was. Was life on Earth perfect all the time?"

She has a point.

Vulrux and Dennox are already in the dining hall, as are about a dozen others, including Sofia and Ryanna. The two Zorahn scientists are nowhere to be seen. Vulrux is sitting next to Sofia, I can't help but notice, and it sends a stab of resentment through me. I tell myself sternly to cut it out.

Both of them get up as soon as they see me, looks of relief on their faces. "You gave us quite a scare, Harper,"

Dennox growls, taking my elbow and leading us away from the curious gazes of the others. "I thought you were taking a nap. When we couldn't find you..." His voice trails off. "Thankfully, Thrax told us where you were."

"I woke up." I narrow my eyes. Like I told Thrax, these two guys aren't the boss of me, and the sooner I point that out to them, the better. I step closer to them and lower my voice since public screaming matches aren't really my style. "Are you saying that I have to tell you whenever I leave the house? Because that's controlling, possessive, and ridiculous."

Vulrux folds his arms over his chest. "You've been in a coma," he retorts. "You're weak. If you accidentally leave the safety of the paths, you could get washed down the mountainside. Yes. Until you're fully recovered, we will accompany you."

I glare at him, but then I remember Viola's words. They've already lost one mate. I can understand their protectiveness; they don't want to lose another. I might be on the fence about this whole mating-bond-thingamabob, but that doesn't mean I have to be a jerk about their concern. Besides, their worry is somewhat justified—I am still pretty shaky on my feet.

"Okay." I give them a small smile. "I didn't mean to worry you."

Their expressions soften. Dennox takes my hand in his. "Are you hungry?" he asks. "Thrax is one of our better cooks."

"I'm starving."

Dinner isn't maggots. If I'm being honest, Dennox is right; the food is pretty good. There's a thick meat and vegetable stew served with an unleavened bread with a nutty taste. Dennox and Vulrux sit on either side of me, and they make sure that I eat two large helpings. "You need to regain your strength," Dennox says when I protest. "Eat."

Their attention is nice, and their presence on either side of me acts as a buffer between me and the others. There are a lot of Draekons. Fourteen of them, in fact. They introduce themselves to me, and I nod and say hello, but I'm sure I won't remember their names or their faces. There better not be a quiz at the end of the night. "What's the matter?" Vulrux says to me under his breath after the fifth Draekon introduces himself.

"I'm not good at names," I whisper back. "I don't want to offend anyone."

He puts his hand on my thigh. "I'll remind you," he promises me. "Don't worry, Harper. We're here for you."

Man, if this is what having mates is like, no wonder Viola's glowing. As I eat, I covertly watch Arax and Nyx. It's obvious that even when they're talking to the others, their attention is on Viola. When her bowl is empty, Nyx silently refills it. When she leans on Arax's shoulder, his expression softens, and he puts his arm around her waist and draws her in.

Would that what it would be like with Vulrux and Dennox?

"Earth to Harper. Come in please."

I look up with a start, and Ryanna sits down opposite me. "Where were you all day?" she asks me. "I came looking for you early this afternoon, but you weren't around."

Vulrux and Dennox are both missing from their seats. Vulrux is standing in a corner, staring out at the rain, holding a cup in his hands—kunnr wine maybe? Dennox is listening to something that Thrax is saying. Lost in my daydreams and the pleasant feeling of fullness after an excellent meal, I hadn't even noticed.

"We went swimming," I reply. *Naked.*

"Nice," she says. She nods in Dennox's direction. "Doesn't say much, does he?"

"Dennox?" I frown at her, puzzled. Dennox wasn't super-chatty today, but he was also the one who agreed to take me to the lake. "Why do you say that?"

"Because he really doesn't," she replies with a roll of her eyes. "Of course," she adds thoughtfully, "When he does speak, people listen." She grins cheekily. "I hope you like the strong, silent type, Harper."

Everyone's acting like the three of us are together. Like it's a done deal, like my consent doesn't matter. Even Ryanna. My good mood evaporates. "Can we talk about something else?" I beg her. "You've been here for more than ten days. How's it been? Are you really okay with living here forever?"

She shrugs, her attention half on me, and half on Thrax. *Hmm. Viola might be right about the two of them.* "I can't think of forever, Harper," she says. "So I don't. I'm taking it one day at a time. There are lots of things about home that I miss, like coffee, but there are also things I don't."

"Like what?"

"Like the constant struggle. I work in retail back home, at a grocery chain in the closest town to us. I've been there since I was fifteen, but I'm still on part-time hours because they don't want to pay benefits. I live on my grandparents' farm, but I've had to sell off pieces of it every year just to keep my head above water." She grimaces. "Whatever I seem to do, it's never enough. The farm is being foreclosed. I volunteered to go to space in desperation; I needed the money to save my family home."

I can relate. My apartment building was in a very dodgy part of Los Angeles. Three times a week, cop cars were outside my door, sirens blaring, guns drawn, looking for low-level drug dealers. Once, there was even a bomb scare in the apartment next to mine. I'd have loved to move to a nicer neighborhood, but I was a teacher, and that was all I could afford with my salary.

Ryanna gives me a steady look. "What was I fighting for? A roof over my head? Arax moved out without complaint and gave us his home. Food and drink? Here it is, offered with generosity. Medical? Vulrux has spent hours by your bedside in the last ten days." Her lips twitch. "Although he might have had ulterior motives."

I ignore that last comment. "You're not sad or angry?"

"I'm keeping busy," she replies. "I can either sit around and feel sorry for myself, or I can make myself useful."

"What is there to do?" In the space of a day, the rainfall has become part of the background noise. "Aren't you terribly cooped up?"

"A little," she admits. "But there's lots to keep me occupied. There's wood to chop. The roofs are made of a kind of tree bark, but they need to be woven, and they're replaced every year. There are knives to carve." Her eyes shine with excitement. "That's the bit I like the best. Thrax is teaching me how to throw them. In the dry season, I want to go hunting."

She leans forward and lowers her voice. "Every single person here was exiled from their home, Harper. The instant they tested positive for the Draekon mutation, they were thrown into quarantine. None of them got a chance to say goodbye to their families or their loved ones. Can you imagine how awful that would have been?" She bites her lower lip. "Given what they went through, I can't complain too much about missing my caffeine fix."

Maybe it's because everyone is on their sixteenth day on

this planet, and I'm just experiencing my first, but Viola, Sofia, and Ryanna don't seem resigned to being here, and they aren't miserable and pouting. In fact, they're rising to the challenge.

Time to stop acting like a spoiled princess.

I finish talking to Ryanna, and then I get up and join Vulrux in his corner. He seems distracted. "Are you okay?" I ask him. "Is something bothering you?"

He looks up with a wry twist of his lips. "Am I that easy to read?"

I put my arm around his waist without even thinking about it, and he stiffens. I flush and try to draw away, but he stops me. "Stay," he requests. "Normally, I like the calm of the rains. This season, however, I cannot wait for the downpour to end."

I get the sense that there's more to his statement than restlessness, but I don't probe. Dennox watches us from across the room, his expression unreadable. When I catch his eye, I beckon him over, but he shakes his head and stays where he is.

VULRUX'S HOUSE, like all the others, isn't huge. There are two square rooms, a wide wrap-around porch, and a larger-than-expected bathroom, with a Draekon-sized tub in it. "You have a bathtub?" I say, dumbstruck. "With hot water?"

He raises his eyebrow. "You weren't expecting one?"

"No," I confess. "Your camp is a weird mix of modern and primitive." Too late, I wonder if I've offended the two men, but neither look annoyed by my tactless comment. "How can the water be warm?"

"A contained fire, insulation from our space pod and *kunnr* reeds for pipes," Dennox replies readily. Back in the dining area, his mood seemed quite dark, but he seems to be in better spirits now. "We're lucky. Odix is a student of ancient civilizations, and Strax and Dazix are builders. The three of them are responsible for our creature comforts."

Vulrux hands me a towel. "Would you like to use the tub?"

Heck yes. A hot bath *and* clean underwear from my luggage? Things are definitely looking up. "I'd love to," I reply, taking the towel from him. "Thank you."

"You have nothing to thank me for, Harper." Vulrux seems to be on the verge of saying something else, but he changes his mind. He looks at my bulging suitcase. "I'll clear some room on the shelves for your possessions," he says instead.

I wish I knew what was going on. Both men are acting like there's something on their minds. Perhaps, after spending some time in my company, they're rethinking things. I was in a committed relationship with Tom, but once he'd met Megan, he stopped paying attention to me. Maybe Vulrux and Dennox want to upgrade mates as well, the way Tom had done.

So what, Harper? You don't even know these two guys. You survived Tom breaking up with you; this is nothing compared to that.

But the sinking feeling in my heart is real. "That'd be nice," I tell Vulrux, fighting the sudden swell of emotion. "Thank you again." Then I run into the bathroom before I burst into tears in front of them and embarrass myself forever.

I SOAK in the herbal-scented water for what seems like hours. On a small shelf next to the tub, there's a bowl of an oily liquid that I correctly assume is soap and a stack of coarse woven washcloths.

Dipping it in the liquid, I run it over my body. The slight roughness of the cloth causes my skin to tingle. My nipples pebble at the friction, sending a sparkle of pleasure through me.

Mmm. I'm alone, and while the bath is doing a great job at draining away my stress, I know one other thing that works even better. I can't even remember when I last touched myself. I'm definitely overdue.

Closing my eyes, I allow my fingers to drift lower.

Two men at once. I wonder what that feels like, especially considering how large the two Draekons are. Will they take it slow, or will they thrust into me in unison?

Stop it, Harper.

But my imagination is on fire, and I can't stop the images that flood through my head. Vulrux's stubble scratching against the soft skin of my inner thighs. Dennox's broad hands squeezing my breasts.

Gah! There must be aphrodisiacs in the alien food because my girly bits have been purring for a while now. Come to think of it, I've been constantly horny since I first woke up and saw my Draekon saviors. Collecting more of the oily soap, I slip a finger between my folds. Instantly, my hips jerk forward, asking for more.

Holy crap, I'm already so close. It was never like this with Tom. He always complained...

No, stop, I tell myself firmly. Don't think of your ex right now. Don't think of anyone. Just get in, get your orgasm, get off. Don't think of a guy. Especially not Vulrux and Dennox's sexy bronze bodies, water streaming from their tattooed muscles as they beckon me into the underground lake.

Oops. Too late.

My fingers circle the sweet spot alongside my clit. I don't waste any time teasing my arousal; there's no need. My naked swimming session with the two hottest guys in the galaxy has more than stoked the fire.

They've been sweet and attentive, helping me down the stairs. Protective, sitting on either side of me, making sure I had plenty to eat. And the way they'd reacted when I'd pressed up against them in the lake, trying to get away from the water snake? There had been heat in their eyes. I'd felt wanted, sexy.

A little cry escapes me, and I clamp my mouth shut. *Gotta rub this out on stealth mode, Harper. Don't want the guys to hear and rush in to help me.* Judging from the half-mast hard-ons they were sporting in the water, they'd be only too happy to give me a hand. A shiver runs through me at the thought of the two men leaning over me, their gazes filled with lust. It would be so easy to call out and—

No, Harper. Don't think of them.

But I can't stop. A few more strokes and my orgasm is on the horizon. My fingers move faster as I imagine Vulrux's head between my legs. Dennox's big hands squeezing my breasts, his thumbs teasing my nipples. I remember the way their eight pack abs ripple with every movement, the way their huge cocks swing between their muscled legs. They're so damn big that I wonder if I can even get my hand around them when they're hard. What will dragon dick feel like against me? Inside me?

My orgasm hits, shockwaves pulsing through me. A loud moan rolls from my mouth. My muscles clench over and over, squeezing on air, begging for giant dragon dick. A final gasp and my head falls back against the tub with a clunk.

I have never come so fast, or so hard.

Or so loud. Shit. I wasn't quiet at all. What if Dennox and Vulrux overheard me?

They did.

The door to the bathroom crashes open, and Vulrux rushes in, Dennox at his heels. "I heard you cry out," he says, and then his eyes take in the entire scene. My flushed face. My right hand positioned between my legs. My erect nipples.

A slow smile breaks out over his face. "We're your mates, Harper," he says. "It is our duty to tend to your needs. *All of them.*"

10

Dennox:

I can smell her arousal, and it wakes the dragon inside, driving the beast wild with lust. *Take her,* it demands. *Touch her. Possess her.*

I take a step forward, driven by instinct. "We will make you moan with pleasure, *diya*," I growl. "All you have to do is ask."

Vulrux places a cautionary hand on my shoulder. I want to tell him not to worry. I'm a soldier of the Zorahn Empire. I've been tortured by rebel armies. I've been wounded and broken and maimed, and I have never once betrayed my word.

Harper bites her lower lip. She doesn't speak, but I don't think she's afraid. Though she's moved her hand from between her legs, she's made no move to cover her breasts. Her nipples are hard, and I ache to capture her rosy tips between my lips.

The seconds tick by. The shimmering gold threads that connect us seem to strengthen in the silence. For long years, my dragon has lied dormant, waiting for a chance to break free. This woman from a distant and unknown planet holds the key to my salvation.

Finally, she speaks. "I can't," she whispers, not meeting our eyes. "It's too soon."

I take a deep breath, trying to push aside the disappointment that floods through me. She's right. Harper Boyd doesn't feel the call of the mating bond the way Vulrux and I do. She doesn't feel the constant tug on our souls, the all-consuming need to be one with her.

"Of course," I reply. I turn around and prepare to leave, but her voice stops me. "Dennox? Vulrux?" she calls out. "Stop for a minute, please? Both of you?"

I wait as she searches for words. Finally, she looks at us. "I'd love to go swimming again tomorrow if the two of you would take me," she says softly. She swallows. "Not just because Arax demands that we spend time together." Her face flushes. "But because I want to."

"Of course," I reply, my heart beating faster in my chest. She's not rejecting us outright. She wants our company. She just needs time. And time is the one thing we have plenty of.

TEN DAYS PASS. Every morning, the three of us eat together and then descend the stairs to the underground lake. We swim together, Harper insisting on wearing a strange garment called a 'swimsuit' that clings to her body but leaves her legs and arms bare. "I don't understand," I tell her, puzzled. "Are you afraid that something will bite your insides?"

Her fair cheeks turn pink. "You're so casual about nudity," she murmurs. "On Zoraht, does everyone walk around with their bits and bobs dangling out all the time?"

"No, but we do swim naked," Vulrux replies. "The cool touch of water against warm skin is one of life's greatest pleasures. Why do you deny yourself?"

Her reply is barely audible. "I'm not sure."

She's not talking about her 'swimsuit' anymore, and we all know it. The attraction grows harder to resist every day. My dragon grows restless at my refusal to complete the mating bond. Vulrux feels the same tension.

And Harper? Maybe I'm imagining it, but I'm convinced Harper's attracted to us too. She's just afraid to take the first step.

~

Harper:

I'm about ready to scream with frustration. I'd give anything to go back to that moment when I told Vulrux and Dennox I needed more time. Because the two dragons have taken me at my word, and they've backed off. Entirely.

Which *totally* sucks.

Every day, we go swimming, but there's no inappropriate flirting. There are no offers to take care of me and meet *all* my needs. In fact, for almost two weeks, they haven't touched me at all. Not even casually.

Confession: I want them. I want to feel their touch. I'm like the cat that keeps pawing at the door, and the moment the door is opened, has no interest in going outside. Yes, I kept saying that I didn't want to be stuck with Vulrux and Dennox, but you know what? Not true.

So now I have to put my big-girl panties on and tell them I want them, and I don't know how to lead up to that conversation. I guess I could strip off my swimsuit—that's one heck of a hint—but I have a sneaking suspicion that even that won't work.

What will work is honesty, but I'm too chicken for that.

I decide to drop another hint. "Tell me about Zoraht," I say. That's a lame opening line, but I have a plan.

Vulrux's lips twitch. "We've spent much of the last week talking about Zoraht," he replies. "You must be quite bored of the homeworld by now."

"Not really." To be honest, I'm fascinated by their lives. Palace intrigues and confrontations in the Senate wars waged on distant worlds—Vulrux and Dennox's lives before exile were very different from my own, and I could listen to them talk about it for days on end.

Right now though, my intentions are decidedly impure. "Tell me about sex," I say boldly. I'm sitting on a flat rock, dipping my toes in the cool water. Dennox is lying on his back next to me, his hands behind his head.

Vulrux pulls himself out of the lake. Drops of water sluice off his body, and I can't help but ogle the sight.

Like a lot of people who lived in Los Angeles, Tom had aspirations to be an actor. He used to spend hours in the gym, lifting weights and doing pushups so he could be in Hollywood shape, but he never looked half as good as the two Draekons in front of me. These guys look ready for the cover of a men's workout magazine. Forget six packs. They've got eight packs. Maybe ten.

"What about it?" Dennox turns his head toward me, his eyes amused.

"Tell me about the first time you had sex." My cheeks heat as soon as I ask the question. Oh God, what if they're virgins? That'd be seriously awkward.

Vulrux's eyes darken, and his voice turns silky. "That's a very intimate question, Harper."

The air between us stills. This is it, Harper. Now or never.

"Is it?" I whisper. "Are you going to answer?"

Dennox sits up. "Maybe." His gaze is on me, focused and intense. I feel my nipples harden under his attention. The fabric of my swimsuit has never felt thinner, and I've never felt more conscious about my nakedness underneath.

"So curious," Vulrux says, his expression turning predatory. I shiver as his gaze rakes over my body. "Very well, Harper. I'll go first. When I hit puberty, a pleasure coach was hired to make sure I learned how to satisfy a woman."

Whoa. Every once in a while, I forget that Vulrux and Dennox are aliens. Their planet, their culture, their customs are completely different. I'm not sure if I'm horrified or intrigued. "A pleasure coach?" My voice sounds strangled. "Is that typical for Zorahn?"

"Only among the Highborn," Dennox says, sounding amused. "The rest of us learn our skills the old-fashioned way. Through practice."

Since the idea of Dennox *practicing* on numerous women sends an uncomfortable tendril of jealousy through me, I focus on Vulrux. "What did your pleasure coach teach you?"

His fingers caress my jaw. "I could tell you," he says softly. "Or I could show you."

My heartbeat accelerates. "Show me..."

With a smile that crinkles the edges of his eyes, Vulrux moves closer. My breathing quickens and I sit up straighter, and he makes a protesting noise in his throat. "Don't move, *diya.*"

"*Diya*?" Oh God, the look of intense need on their faces sets my pulse racing. I've waited so long for this moment. For days, I've been fantasizing about them, hoping they'd make a move. Now, it's happening. "What does that mean?"

"Precious one." Dennox answers.

Precious one. A lump forms in my throat as I stare at them. It's not just a term of endearment. It's the way they've treated me from the moment I woke up.

Vulrux seats himself behind me, his long, bare legs on either side of mine.

"Vulrux, what... what are you doing?"

"Showing you what I was taught." His hands skim down my arms, and I tense involuntarily. "Relax," he soothes, drawing me back against him with an arm around my middle. "Rest your head against me."

I do as he asks, and he shifts so I'm leaning into the crook of his arm. His big hand brushes my hair from my shoulder and then wraps around the base of my neck and lightly squeezes. Not like he's choking me, more like a firm, claiming grip.

"Um, I'm not sure—" My voice trails off as he starts to massage my shoulder, his thumb sliding over the tight muscle. All the fight goes out of me as he gives me the best massage of my life, focusing on my neck and shoulders. I used to get massages regularly after swimming, but not like this. Vulrux seems to know just how to soothe the stress right out of me. And man, do I have a lot of stress. Crashing a spaceship on an alien planet will do that to a girl.

Vulrux's fingers knead me expertly. I let out a moan.

This is way better than my own attempts at self-care. This is perfect. Or it would be if Dennox weren't watching us with a raised brow.

"Is this how a Highborn fucks?" The dark-haired Draekon's tone says *'you're doing it wrong.'*

I stifle back a laugh. Vulrux is unfazed. "This is how we

begin," he says. "A woman's neck is very sensitive. I hold her life," his voice lowers, his palm sliding to my front and his fingers encircling my neck, "In my hands."

My insides quiver, but my pussy is thrilled. Apparently, I like having a guy's hand around my neck. Vulrux doesn't leave it there but gently works the tight tendons, working on relaxing me as if he has all the time in the world.

"Touching her this way, without immediately groping her breasts or cunt, gives her time to relax," Vulrux continues to lecture, his deep voice rumbling. "Takes her thoughts away. Allows her to slip into pleasure."

It's working.

Dennox grunts as if he's not convinced. "It's okay, Dennox." I give him a lazy smile. "You'll get your turn."

His lips curl into a smile. "And when I do," he says, looking straight at me, his voice whiskey-smooth, "I'll show you how a soldier fucks."

My pussy clenches with a rush of pleasure.

"Not yet," Vulrux orders. "No fucking today. This is all for you, Harper."

"Wait, what?" I start, but Vulrux digs in deeper, releasing a knot I didn't even know was there. I melt into a puddle. I was hoping to feel them inside me, but at this point, I'd take anything. Vulrux's clever fingers ease down the straps of my bathing suit, baring my chest, but I barely register it.

"He's right," Dennox agrees. "This is all for you." He gets to his feet and moves closer to me, his hard cock jutting from between his legs. I'm pretty sure my mouth is open, and I'm drooling. But when he gets close, he only sits down in front of me, pulls my feet into my lap, and starts massaging them too. "Not just this time. *Every time.* Our focus is always on you."

Mini. Orgasm.

My eyes roll back in my head. "Oh God," I whimper. "This is so good."

"She's praying?" Dennox asks Vulrux, looking puzzled.

"Human women sometimes do that, when they feel immense pleasure. I have heard this from Arax and Nyx."

"More rubbing, less talking," I try to say, but it comes out a barely intelligible mumble. Dennox's thumbs work my arches, and Vulrux has taken to massaging my scalp. He moves my hair aside and places a gentle kiss on the curve of my shoulder.

I shiver. He does it again, his lips doing delicious things to my insides. I feel the press of his lips all the way down in my pussy.

"Someone got an A in anatomy," I murmur, as he continues to light my body up with each kiss at the base of my neck. Fuck, this is so good. I feel like I should be writing a thank-you note to Vulrux's pleasure coach.

"Shh. Close your eyes," Vulrux orders. "Surrender to pleasure, Harper." He pulls me flush against him, so my bottom is cradled in his lap. A comfortable seat, even with the long, hard bar of his cock pressing into me.

I lean back against his chest, and his hands come around to stroke my collarbone, teasing just above my breasts. Under my wet bathing suit, my nipples tingle, and my breath catches in anticipation.

"Once she is relaxed, it is time to touch new places."

"Breasts?" Dennox asks.

"Not yet."

I almost laugh at Dennox's disappointed grunt. He must be a boob man. Boob alien. Boob dragon?

A giggle escapes me. Dennox cocks a brow. "Are you laughing at me?" He lifts my leg and props it on his shoulder. Turning his head, he presses a kiss under my knee.

"Oooh," I half-whimper, half-squeal. Who'd have thought the back of my knee was an erogenous spot? Not me.

He does it again, and again, turning his head this way and that to scrape his stubble on my sensitive skin.

I jerk. "That tickles—"

"Does it?" He holds my leg tighter as I struggle, his eyes crinkling as he smiles at me. "This is my revenge for you laughing at me."

"I wasn't—"

His smile widens. "I like the way you laugh, Harper. I wish to hear it again." He lifts my other leg on his opposite shoulder and nuzzles it too.

My pussy is dripping. There's probably a puddle on the rock.

Vulrux, not to be left out, latches onto the tender spot between my neck and shoulder, and sucks hard. I feel the pull of his lips all the way between my legs. "Oh God," I whimper again.

Dennox bites my calf lightly. Vulrux slides his hand down between my breasts, still avoiding my aching mounds. His palm heats my skin as he pushes my swimsuit even lower. I raise my hips and let him and Dennox ease the garment off.

Both men's eyes drink me in greedily. Dennox keeps massaging my calves, working slowly up my legs. Vulrux's fingers trail everywhere, dipping into the hollow in front of my hip bones, stroking back up my side to trace my collarbone. Every so often both men pause to press their lips to my skin.

I'm in Paradise, completely lost to the two mouths and four hands working up and down my body. They touch every part of me. Every part, that is, except my breasts and clit, which they leave alone. Maddening dragons. Enough foreplay. I need more.

"Fuck," I beg, lifting my hips toward their fingers, "fuck me."

"Not today Harper," Vulrux says firmly. His fingers trail around my breasts, the whisper-soft strokes stimulating them without touching.

"Argh," I open my mouth to curse, and Dennox drops down between my legs, kissing up my thighs. My legs clamp together, but he holds them apart. Vulrux wraps his hand around my right breast and squeezes just as Dennox stabs his tongue into me.

I almost explode.

Dennox thrusts again and again, and it drives me wild. Vulrux's slow teasing combined with Dennox's firm touch? The combination of the two of them is going to kill me. My muscles quiver and tremble under the assault of Dennox's skillful tongue. My insides tighten and twist, and I throw my head back and plead for more. My orgasm dances just out of reach. I'm close, so close.

"My turn. I wish to taste her."

I groan with frustration as Dennox takes his mouth off my pussy, and the two men switch places. I'm too dazed to move. Not that I want to escape. I'd have to be made to want to run away from this. Why have I been resisting?

Vulrux settles himself between my legs. His strong hands close around my thighs, holding them open. Bending his head, he nibbles my pussy, and I squirm restlessly as desire overtakes me.

"Stay still," he growls. He holds my hips so I can't move, and he laps me up and down. His tongue finds the sweet spot beside my clit and flicks it over and over, a maddening cadence that has my hips dancing.

Just as I'm getting close, he slides his hand under me and probes a finger into my ass.

I explode, screaming and bucking into Vulrux's face. Dennox's hands cover my breasts, his thumbs strumming my nipples as I spasm over and over. My cries echo around the lake.

Crap, I hope no one else heard me.

Dennox cradles me against his hard body, holding me as I bask in the afterglow of my orgasm. Vulrux comes close, offering me a drink of water from his cupped palms. I wet my throat, and he pulls me into a hug. As I bury my face in his chest, his hands roam, finding my ass and squeezing my bottom cheeks.

Definitely an ass draekon.

"Holy fuck," I say as soon as I find my voice. "That was incredible. Your pleasure coach was certainly good at her job."

Vulrux's grin stretches from ear to ear.

Smug alien. I'll show him. Twining my arms around his shoulders, I pull him close and kiss him hard. I want to see them unravel with the same pleasure they gave me. I want to feel their cocks move inside me, and I want to feel the hard press of their bodies against mine.

After a startled pause, he cups the back of my neck, holding me still for his plundering tongue. He's not patient now. His kiss is deep and possessive, and I close my eyes as another wave of lust washes over me.

The second he lets me go, Dennox tugs my hair lightly and takes his turn to claim my lips. My hands rest on two muscled chests, one hand on Vulrux, the other on Dennox. My palm vibrates as a deep purr rumbles through their giant, muscled forms.

Somehow, I know the source of the sound.

Dragon.

"YOU NEVER TOLD me about your first time," I accuse Dennox lazily as we lie on the rocks. I guess we should head back up, but I'm too sated to move.

He laughs. "We were otherwise distracted," he replies. "I was taken right after puberty to join the Zoraken. Sex was not permitted during training; it was only a distraction. I didn't feel the pleasure of a woman's touch until after my first battle. It was the Liberation of Kraush. The planet was occupied by rogue slavers. The Zoraken got rid of them." His mouth widens into a grin as he remembers. "The citizens of Kraush were *very* grateful."

Vulrux sits up suddenly. "You said the Zoraken are mind-wiped after every battle. How can you remember the Liberation of Kraush?"

Dennox's face goes white. I look from one man to the other.

Something's just happened. Something momentous.

11

Vulrux:

We climb the stairs silently, each of us lost in our thoughts.

So much is happening. Dennox's memories might be coming back. Harper knows about the mindwipes, but I don't know if she realizes the significance of what's happening. If Dennox can remember the Liberation of Kraush, he might also eventually remember how he ended up at the Crimson Citadel.

Dennox wants to be certain that he isn't a monster. Me? I just want to know what happened so I can get closure on the past.

"I'm really getting in good shape," Harper says as she climbs. "The first day, every muscle in my body was screaming in protest by the time I was back at camp. Another weird thing? I don't have a timer, and the lake isn't exactly set up for laps, but I swear I'm swimming faster too."

I exchange a wary look with Dennox. It's obvious what's happening; the same thing happened with Viola when she mated with Arax and Nyx. In Harper's case, the blood transfusion is causing her body to change. "It's the Draekon genes," I reply.

She stops in her tracks. I brace myself for her anger, but after a moment of thought, she shrugs philosophically. "Well, you did warn me," she says. "And I like being stronger and faster." Her expression turns intrigued. "At some point, will I become a dragon? That'd be awesome."

I laugh out loud. At almost every turn, Harper surprises me. She has a resilience about her that is very attractive. In camp, she's friendly and cheerful, taking the time to get to know every single person. She volunteers for chores and does her share without complaint. She's curious about everything, and she's genuinely interested in our lives, both back on the homeworld and on the prison planet.

"Only men with the Draekon mutation transform into dragons," I tell her. "Sorry."

"Of course." She rolls her eyes. "Even on an alien planet, a glass ceiling."

I frown in confusion at the unfamiliar phrase. "Never mind," she murmurs. "Why are there no female dragons?"

"I don't know," I reply honestly. "The Draekons were mostly wiped out during the Great Rebellion, and any mention of them was erased from the ThoughtVaults. That was a thousand years ago. Arax, as Firstborn, was able to access the secret archives, but there wasn't much detail in them."

Harper chews on her lower lip as she digests that.

Beirax believes the Draekon race is poised on the edge of rebirth. Is he right? I'm inclined to doubt the scientist. He's got all the hallmarks of a fanatic, and I can't trust him to be objective.

"The whole thing sucks," she says. "You guys got exiled from your home, and you don't even know why?"

Her concern warms my heart. "We'll know soon enough what the Draekons are capable of," I tell her. "Arax and Nyx can transform at will now. Once the rains stop, they'll be able to test their abilities."

"Not just Arax and Nyx," she says, her face coloring. "Won't you transform too?"

If we complete the mating bond.

But that isn't as simple as it appears because it isn't just about desire. I'm hiding Beirax's revelations from Harper. A small, base part of me wants to forget about the cloakship and take what Harper freely offers, but I won't allow myself to do that.

I'm blurring the line between right and wrong. Guilt about drugging Beirax fills me. I should have told everyone about what I discovered ten days ago, but I didn't. I've kept shamefully silent.

Before we go any further, Harper deserves to know the truth.

I hesitate, wondering how to formulate my reply. Dennox gives me a sharp look, and I shake my head imperceptibly. "I expect so," I reply at last. "I don't want to take you for granted, Harper."

She flushes. "I don't know if you noticed," she says, "but I had a really good time down there. I think it's safe to say that sex is a foregone conclusion."

~

Harper:

Confession time. I'm a little freaked out by the Draekon mutation thingy. The idea of an organism inside me rewriting my genetic code, tweaking and fine-tuning until it gets to a better, more perfect version of Harper? It reminds me of the Cybermen in Doctor Who. *You will be upgraded.* Or, worse, the scene in Alien, the one where the baby alien bursts out of that guy's belly.

Don't be ridiculous, Harper.

From what Vulrux just told me, nobody knows anything about the Draekons, not even Arax. The scientists created them, and the scientists destroyed them, and when Draekon genes show up in the population, the scientists just sweep it under the rug by exiling them.

The scientists. *Of course.* The fourteen exiles might not know anything about the mutation, but I bet that the two scientists stuck on the prison planet do.

I'm going to need to talk to Raiht'vi. As soon as I can.

You know the women who claim they have headaches to avoid sex? I never thought I'd be one of them, but the moment we reach the camp, I turn to Dennox and Vulrux. "I'm not feeling too good," I fib, feeling a stab of guilt at their concerned expressions. "My head hurts. It's nothing a nap won't solve."

Liar, liar, pants on fire.

"What about food, *diya?*" Dennox asks, his hand cradling my cheek. "Should we get you something?"

I shake my head. "I'm fine. I'm still stuffed from breakfast."

Vulrux looks like he's going to probe further, but he's

distracted by the sight of an approaching man. It's Rorix, the Draekon who was in a coma for three months. I wonder if Thrax teased him about my own quicker recovery. If so, Rorix has never given any indication. The man is perpetually cheerful and good-natured.

He greets us with a friendly smile before turning to Vulrux. "Zorux cut himself while carving a knife," he says. "It's nothing serious. Do you have a salve for him?"

"You don't think anything short of a full *enrak* attack is serious," Vulrux replies with a roll of his eyes. "I'll come along and take a look." He gives me an uncertain gaze. "Are you sure you're okay, Harper?"

"Yes." I put my hand on his arm. Mmm. Nice biceps. Really nice. Firm. I picture Vulrux holding me down as he kisses me, and my stomach does a funny little jump. I can't wait to make love to them.

Vulrux disappears with Rorix. Once he leaves, Dennox turns to me. "If you need me, I'll be in my house."

His expression is pensive. In fact, come to think of it, he's barely said anything since he mentioned the Liberation of Kraush. "Is everything okay, Dennox? You look shaken."

His shoulders lift in a small shrug. "I've been mind-wiped eighteen times, Harper. I thought my memories were lost forever. To find out that I might be able to regain them..." He takes a deep breath. "I don't know what to feel."

I nicknamed Dennox Mr. Linebacker when I first met him. He's big, strong and fearless. The rare moment of vulnerability takes me by surprise. I stand on tiptoe and brush my lips against his. "If you want to talk about it, I'm here."

He squeezes my hand. "Thank you. But I need to be alone."

"Of course." I stare at his back as he walks away, my

heart sinking in my chest. Dennox and Vulrux have told me all about their lives, with one exception. They've never talked about their first mate. *Ever.*

Now Dennox doesn't want to talk about his memories.

I stand outside Vulrux's front door for a long time, staring at the rain. If I'm being perfectly honest, I really like Dennox and Vulrux. They're hot. They're nice. They treat me like some kind of princess. And umm, not to be too crass, but the stuff we did down in the lake? Whoa. I have no words.

I might even be falling in love.

But what if they've never gotten over their first mate?

I MAKE my way down the path to Zorux's house, where Raiht'vi and Beirax are recuperating. As I walk, my mind spins in a thousand different directions. The hanky-panky with Dennox and Vulrux. Dennox's memories returning, and what that might mean for us. Vulrux's odd hesitation when we talked about the two of them transforming into dragons.

Beirax or Raiht'vi?

Let's see. Beirax crashed our spaceship on the prison planet, killing Janet outright and condemning the rest of us to spend the remainder of our lives here. Raiht'vi, on the other hand, might not be the queen of charm, but she told Vulrux and Dennox how to save my life.

Raiht'vi it'll be.

I knock on Zorux's front door. Nyx opens it, and I blink at him, surprised. "What are you doing here?"

He snorts. "It's my turn to feed the two ungrateful idiots in there," he says. "Why the two of them can't eat in the dining area like the rest of us, I don't understand. Then again, they'll probably just glower at everyone." He gives me a quizzical look. "And what are *you* doing here?"

Is Nyx going to give me a hard time? "I'm here to see Raiht'vi," I reply.

He steps aside. "First door on the right."

Well, that was easy.

Raiht'vi's door is ajar. She's awake, half-propped up on her bed, fiddling with a thick bluish metal band on her wrist. When I knock, she looks up and seems surprised to see me.

"Can I come in?"

Her expression turns guarded. "Yes."

I sit down on the solitary chair in the room and get right to the point. "When Vulrux and Dennox gave me their blood, it cured me, but it also passed on the Draekon mutation to me."

She nods curtly.

"My body's changing," I tell the scientist. "I'm getting stronger. I can swim faster." I take a deep breath. "What else can happen?"

"I don't know."

Her reply is evasive, and I'm positive she knows more than she's telling. "Are you sure?" I press her. "You were the one who told Vulrux and Dennox about the curative properties of Draekon blood. Are you positive you don't know what might end up happening to me?"

This time, she gives me a dismissive look. "I don't share everything I know with humans," she says, her lips curled into a scowl. "Or with Draekons."

Her hands clench into fists. On the *Fehrat 1*, only a few weeks ago, Raiht'vi seemed invincible. Now though? She's trying to stay strong, but she's stranded on this world as much as I am. I don't have any close family—none of the women who were chosen to fly to Zorahn do—but she might. Maybe she had a husband, children. Maybe she's homesick and has to hide it under a veneer of strength.

I realize I know nothing about the Zorahn woman. She's got to be feeling the same tumult of emotions that I've been struggling with since I woke up from my coma, and she doesn't even have the company of the others to cheer her up.

Honestly, I feel a little sorry for her.

I pull my chair closer to her bed. "Sofia's the kind and gentle one," I tell her. "I'm much blunter. My mom used to accuse me of being tactless. When my friends in high school would call me to whine about their loser boyfriends, I wouldn't make sympathetic noises. I'd tell them to dump the assholes."

"What are you chattering about, human?"

"The name's Harper." I give her what I hope is a friendly smile. "Should I call you Raiht'vi, or do you have a nickname?"

The Zorahn scientist looks at me as if I've grown a second head. "Hey, we're stuck here," I tell her. "Might as well be friends, right?"

Raiht'vi has a great resting bitch face. The look she gives me is withering, but I don't allow my smile to dim. Finally, she relents with a sigh of impatience. "You can call me Raiht'vi."

We're making progress. "Awesome." I draw a deep breath. "Look," I tell her honestly, "we're all in this together. Beirax got us in this mess, but there's no need for the rest of us to be at each other's throats." God, I feel like Viola. Any moment now, we'll be holding hands and singing Kumbaya.

She snorts derisively. "Your human lifespan is short," she says. "I can never be friends with the Draekons. There's too much history between us."

"Between you and the Draekons?"

Her body goes still. "Between the scientists and the Draekons," she says at last, her voice wary. "The scientists created the Draekons and sent them to battle against their will. When Kannix gave the order to annihilate the Draekons, it was the scientists that created the diseases that wiped them out. I can assure you, Harper Boyd, that no matter what you think, the Draekons and I can *never* be friends."

I give her an incredulous look. "The stuff you're talking about happened a thousand years ago."

"It doesn't matter. Do you think Arax has forgotten that it is a scientist that tested him for the Draekon mutation? The mutation that stripped him from the throne?"

I feel out of my depth. "I don't think Arax bears you any harm."

Her retort is immediate and predictable. "You know nothing." She laughs bitterly. "Beirax, that misguided idiot, wants to bring the Draekons back. The madmen in the Order of the Crimson Night believe that the Draekons can be controlled. Fools, all of them. They forget the most important thing. You can control an animal, but the Draekons are sentient." She pauses, and her next words are almost inaudible. "And they have much to be angry about."

We sit in silence for a few minutes. I'm trying to think of what to say next. Raiht'vi is talking about events that happened a thousand years ago as if it were yesterday, but staying stuck in the past solves nothing. If I were going to do that, I'd be sitting in a corner, rocking back and forth, moaning about chocolate and coffee.

God, I miss a good latte. I'd kill for a cappuccino machine. And Internet access. If I had Internet access, I'd be posting pictures of hot guys with eight-pack abs all day. Who needs Tumblr when you have Draekons?

Finally, Raiht'vi breaks the quiet, probably in order to get me out of her room. "The Draekon mutation shouldn't affect you adversely," she says. "Humans are a compatible species."

Hallelujah, she's talking. "If I get pregnant, the baby isn't going to burst out of me, right? It's not going to leave a big, gaping, hole in my stomach?"

Aliens. Should have never watched that movie as a teenager. Scared the crap out of me.

Raiht'vi gives me an 'are you freaking kidding me' look, the kind my teachers used to reserve for me when I said something exceptionally stupid. "There is nothing that should prevent you from carrying a child to term," she says finally.

I heave a sigh of relief. There's no need to freak out; there's nothing to worry about. There's nothing to stop me from sexing it up with my two hot men.

It's taken me more than two weeks to get to this point, two weeks in which the attraction has simmered, the fire slowly being stoked, two weeks in which my doubts have disappeared under the weight of my need.

I don't want to wait anymore. I'm ready.

12

Dennox:

I sense Harper's disappointment when I tell her I want to be alone, but I cannot help it.

The dragon clamored for more, demanded that Vulrux and I plunge into her soft, willing body and take her, claim her, make her ours. *Until I remembered the Liberation of Kraush.*

As we climb the stairs, it seems like a dam has burst in my head. Images tumble out, clearer than they've ever been before. I remember our ship landing in the main square of Padris, Kraush's capital city. For the Zoraken, Kraush was a minor skirmish. Not so for the Kraush, who viewed the two companies of Zoraken as saviors. Danae was one of them. Her deep golden eyes had sparkled with gratitude as she served the hungry and thirsty troops. As the evening went on, and more pints of Padris' finest *firna* were consumed, her expression had changed to lust. She'd taken my hand and led me up a set of stairs...

That memory had been wiped as soon as the Zoraken

returned to their bases, but it's come back to me. Eighteen battles. Kraush. Senish. Gaarven. The hellholes of Remousi. And of course, there was the last battle. Adrash.

It's Adrash that I'm thinking of as I make my way back to my house. Pouring myself a cup of *kunnr* wine, I sit on the porch and watch the rain. The battlefield had been gray. Bodies were strewn everywhere. In death, the Zoraken lay side by side with the maroon-robed Adrashian techmages.

We'd holed up in a bombed house in the high-walled city of Karhm, waiting for reinforcements. Our supplies were running low, and three of my soldiers were badly wounded. As dangerous as it was, I'd decided to head out to the battlefield, hoping to find a med-kit among the fallen.

Someone had followed me.

A cold sweat breaks out on my skin, and though the air is warm, I shiver involuntarily as the memories unfold in my mind. I'd realized I had a shadow almost as soon as I'd stepped out, but I'd kept going, hoping to lure him or her into a trap.

I'd walked into an ambush. Six highly trained techmages had surrounded me, their staffs glowing. I'd drawn my weapon and stood my ground, prepared to die in battle, but one of the techmages had signaled to the others. "Our orders are to bring this one in alive."

Another long-dormant memory surfaces. A gold-tipped needle puncturing the skin of my neck. Bright blue blood trickling out. The tester flashing crimson. "Draekon," the techmages had hissed in unison. "The Zorahn scientists will pay a bounty for him."

The next thing I remember, I'd been in the Crimson Citadel, tied down so I couldn't escape.

A deep shudder of relief passes through me.

I had not been handed over by the Zoraken to the Scientists as punishment for crimes I'd committed. I'd been kidnapped by the Adrashian techmages.

I don't understand why the scientists would ally with the Adrashians, and I don't remember anything that happened to me at the Crimson Citadel, but I know one thing. I'm not a monster.

I'm now free to claim Harper.

Harper:

When I return from talking to Raiht'vi, both Vulrux and Dennox are waiting for me. "Before you start," I warn them, "you only said I had to tell you where I was going *until* I recovered."

Vulrux doesn't crack a smile. "There's something I need to tell you," he says. "It's important."

My heart does a funny little pitter-patter. Vulrux's expression is more serious than I've ever seen it. I give Dennox a sideways glance, but he looks as puzzled as I do.

"What's going on?"

He seems to gather his thoughts. "You already know about our first mate," he says. "Like Dennox, she was being held prisoner by the scientists. One night, some unknown instinct drew me there."

Please don't say you're still in love with her, please don't say you're still in love with her... I don't think I can bear hearing those words from Vulrux. I was miserable when Tom broke up with me, but underneath the pain, I'd known that Tom wasn't a very nice person, and I'd known, as much as I would have denied it then, that I was better off without him.

I won't have any such consolation with Dennox and Vulrux.

"You've already heard that we transformed into dragons when we saw her," he says. "And you know that when we changed, the guards didn't know what to do. They fired at us, but our scales are impenetrable, and their weapons did not hurt us. Then, one of the guards received an order." His hands clench into fists, his knuckles white with pressure. "He turned his weapon on the woman and killed her. The moment she died, Dennox and I transformed back to men."

Vulrux is right; I already know this story. I'd demanded the truth from Viola, and she'd revealed everything. The surprise isn't in the details of the narrative. The surprise is that Vulrux is telling me about it.

"I was exiled immediately after that," he continues. "For years, I burned to know who gave the order that killed her. And then, your spaceship crashed on the prison planet, along with two people that might know the truth."

"Raiht'vi and Beirax?"

He nods. "Indeed. Raiht'vi, in particular, wears white robes, a mark of distinction among the scientists. Only a handful of them earns that honor."

"So you asked her?" I frown at the tall man in front of me. "I can't imagine Raiht'vi telling you anything."

"I didn't expect either scientist to be forthcoming with the truth," he replies with an oddly ashamed look on his face. "But I had to know. Not just for my sake. For Dennox's as well."

Dennox looks sharply at Vulrux. "What did you do?"

"I couldn't bring myself to harm Raiht'vi. Not after what she did for Harper." He stares at the two of us. "So I drugged Beirax."

A shocked squeal erupts from my lips. "What?"

"I'm not proud of it," he says flatly. "I will take the guilt of what I did to my grave. But I don't regret doing it, and if I had to make the same choice over again, I would."

"What did you learn?" Dennox asks intently. "Did you find out why I was there?"

"No. Beirax knew nothing about the underground labs."

Dennox's shoulders slump. I frown at Vulrux. "There's more to this story, isn't there?" I guess. "You said you wanted to talk to me. You found out something connected to us, didn't you?" My voice rises. "Vulrux, tell me."

"Beirax's mission was to determine if the human women would trigger the Draekon transformation," he says. "If he succeeded, he was to carry word back to the Order of the Crimson Night."

He takes a deep breath. "According to Beirax, somewhere out in the jungle," he says, "are the component parts of a Cloakship." He looks at me steadily. "There might be a way off the prison planet, Harper Boyd. There might be a way for you to go back to your planet. To Earth."

I stare at him, shocked and speechless.

"The Draekon mutation has made your body stronger," he says. "If we mate, the effects will accelerate. The mutation will prepare your womb for Draekon young, and you will not be able to bear human children any longer."

He draws a deep breath. "If you mate with us," he concludes, "the effects are permanent."

I look back and forth between the two men. I don't really know what to say.

13

Harper:

Talk about a bombshell revelation.

I stare at Vulrux and Dennox. I don't know what to say. Part of me is celebrating the idea of returning to Earth—chocolate! Coffee! Pizza delivery—but another, much more insistent part of me wants to be sick.

Vulrux kneels down next to me and takes my hand in his. "I know this is a shock to you," he says, his lips twisting into a grimace. "I didn't want our first time together to be under false pretenses, Harper."

"I know." I bite my lower lip. "Do you think Beirax is lying about the ship?"

"No," he says. "But I also don't want you to get your hopes up. Beirax *thinks* that the Order did a supply drop at a site that's two months away by foot. He *believes* there's a locator on the spaceship that will show him the way there. But the locator could be damaged. We could get to the supply site and find out that the parts are unusable. No one in our Exile batch is a technician; we might not be able to put the ship together. Even if we assemble the ship, we might not be able to pilot our way out of the asteroid belt. And finally," he finishes, "we can't set off in search of the supply site until the rains end."

He's right. It's a thread of hope, but a slim thread. I hold my breath as I ask him my next question. "Do you want to go back to Zoraht?"

He shakes his head immediately. "I'm Draekon," he replies. "There's no place for me in the homeworld, and I don't have any desire to change that. I'm content with my life here." He looks at me with heat in his eyes. "I don't want to change anything, Harper," he repeats.

The tight fist around my heart eases. I turn to Dennox. "Did you know about this? This morning, at the lake, both of you appeared reluctant to take things further."

A strange expression flickers over his face. "Harper," he says, "ever since you woke up, I've been fighting my need to claim you. I don't want there to be any doubt about how much I want you."

There's a 'but' in that sentence. I wait for it.

"But," he says, "until today, I held myself back."

"Why?" I whisper.

"Because my memories were missing," he replies. "I'd ended up as a prisoner at the Crimson Citadel. I thought I'd committed an unspeakable crime for the Zoraken to surrender me to the scientists."

Vulrux looks up. "You have your memories back?" he asks intently. "You remember everything?"

Dennox shakes his head. "Not yet. I remember nothing after I arrived at the Citadel, but I do remember the circumstances that led me there. The Zoraken didn't surrender me. I was kidnapped right after the Battle of Adrash. Half a dozen techmages captured me, tested me for the mutation, and collected a bounty from the scientists."

He fixes me with a direct look. "I didn't know what I was capable of, Harper, and couldn't risk hurting you. But now I know that I'll never do that."

Silly Dennox. I could have told him that *days* ago. Vulrux and Dennox have never once pressured me. They've never made me feel uncomfortable or nervous or frightened around them. Ever.

I don't care about some hypothetical future back on Earth. Not when a very real future is in front of me. One with the two hottest men I've ever seen in my life.

Who have some crazy oral skills.

Who make me scream with pleasure.

Whose cocks have made my mouth water from the moment I caught a glimpse of them.

"Do either of you have anywhere to be for the next couple of hours?" I whip my t-shirt over my head, and Dennox and Vulrux's eyes instantly go to my naked breasts. "Because if you don't, I have some ideas of what we can do."

Their eyes flare with heat. "Do you?" Dennox asks silkily. He picks me up and carries me to the bedroom, tossing me on the bed. "Tell us all about it."

His dominance sends a thrill through me. "I'd rather show you," I purr, coming to my knees. I run my palm over his cock through his pants, holding his eyes. I've never been so brazen, I'm emboldened by his open look of need.

"Show me then," he commands, unfastening his pants so I can really look at him. His cock is already jutting out, thick, proud and ready.

Yum.

Vulrux undresses as well. Everywhere I look, it's a feast for the eyes. Bronze skin, every inch covered in muscles, tattoos, and nipples piercings. They're my naughtiest fantasy come to life. And there are two of them. Lucky, *lucky* Harper.

I slide my hand down Dennox's muscled chest, down the tight V leading to his groin. He gasps when I grasp his cock at the base. I smile. Sure enough, as I'd suspected, when I curl my fingers around his thick member, they barely meet.

"Tell me," I ask. "Do Draekons like when their mates lick their cocks?"

"Put your mouth on mine, and find out." The breathless quality of Dennox's voice tells me all I need to know.

Dipping my head, I press a kiss to his hard, hot member. It throbs under my lips. "Harper," Dennox groans. He strokes my cheek, the gentle gesture a contrast to the stark, raw need in his tone.

A thrill runs through me at the way his eyes are clenched shut. Slipping my hand underneath, I caress his balls. They tighten, and his cock rises even more.

I also got an A in anatomy.

I tease Dennox with my lips until he reaches a hand underneath to squeeze my breasts, his grip firm I sit up to give him more access, taking his cock in hand and slowly stroking it.

Vulrux pulls on his cock as he watches. I lick my lips and beckon him closer. Yes, the two men swim naked, and I've seen their cocks before, but this is the first time I've been able to touch. Call me greedy, but I want to feel both of them. After all, it's the Draekon way.

With a curl of his lips, he approaches the bed, slipping behind me. Surprise, surprise, he goes right for my bottom, gripping and massaging my flesh. Dennox keeps playing with my breasts as Vulrux fondles my ass.

I arch my back and enjoy the attention. Two hot, attentive guys, seeing to my every need? *Yes, please.*

Vulrux's lips trail kisses down my neck and shoulder as his finger nudges between my ass cheeks. I'm not a total anal virgin, but the one time Tom ventured there, it was weird and uncomfortable. I never let him do it again.

I make a little noise in protest. Immediately both men stop. "Did we hurt you, *diya?*" Dennox asks.

"No." *Keep touching me.* "I didn't mean to make you stop."

"Does this frighten you?" Vulrux runs his fingers over my bottom. My pussy aches at just that light touch, and a shiver of pure pleasure runs through me. I'm nervous about both of them being in me at the same time, but every instinct tells me I can trust Vulrux and Dennox to make this good for me. Not just good. Amazing.

I make a decision. "No," I say softly. "I know you would never hurt me." I push my ass back into his hand. "Please don't stop."

"I will make it feel good," he promises.

Dennox wastes no time getting back to worshiping my chest. His large hands cup my breasts, offering them up to his mouth. His tongue swirls around my areola before nipping sharply, making me suck in a breath. "You like that, Harper?"

I can only whimper in reply. My insides ache and tighten as Dennox takes turns sucking each nipple between his lips.

Vulrux's finger rims my hole, pressing slowly. It yields under pressure. He must have used some sort of lube or something because it slides right in. The slick, stuffed feeling stirs my arousal up further.

Dennox nips my aching nipples with his teeth, and I shake, gasping, already so close.

"No, Harper," Dennox says, raising his head with a wicked smile. "You will wait for us this time."

"Please," I groan. I'm not above begging, but Dennox stops my mouth with his kiss.

Vulrux presses his lips down my spine, heading—oh no, would he really do that? He nibbles on one ass cheek, then the other. My pussy is dripping, and little mewls of need escape my lips. I thought I had a vivid imagination, but this is hotter than my wildest fantasies.

With a hand on the back of my neck, Dennox guides me to all fours. The tight V of his midriff fills my vision, along with his giant, jutting cock. I've had it with teasing. I open my mouth and take in the broad head, lapping at him.

His precum is thick, with a honey flavor. I taste again—yep, definitely sweet. Holy wow. Sweet and attentive, muscles for days, yummy-tasting precum. Can these guys get any more perfect?

Dennox strokes my hair, his face full of wonder, as if he can't quite believe I'm real.

I flick my tongue over his cock, looking up at him with lust-filled eyes. "So good," I murmur, opening my mouth for more, ready to take his length down my throat and suck him like a Draekon popsicle.

Vulrux lifts my hips and props my bottom up higher. I feel his breath against my inner thighs, then he presses his lips against my skin. He kisses me, soft and slow, as if he has all the time in the world.

Finally, he puts his mouth on my pussy. I gasp as his tongue swipes a path between my pussy lips, and every muscle in my body tightens in response.

My moan vibrates around Dennox's thick cock, and he throws his head back and bites out a curse. Vulrux's licks speed up, lapping up and down my pussy as if he wants to commit the taste of me to his memory His tongue circles my clitoris and I whimper as my insides tighten.

His mouth pulls away, and I'm about to moan in protest when I feel the flared head of his cock at my entrance.

"Yes," I murmur around Dennox' cock. I'm sucking as if my life depends on it, only pausing to gasp for breath when Vulrux pushes inside me.

"Fuck, yes."

With a gentle hand on my back, Vulrux glides in and out, slowly at first, then faster.

It. Feels. Ah. Mazing.

Dennox tugs my hair a little, drawing my attention back to his cock. I lean forward, taking more of his length than I have before to make up for neglecting him.

The two men rock in and out of me, one in my pussy, one in my mouth. My brain tries to keep up with the sensation. System overload. Abandon all thought. My orgasm rises like the tide, threatening to engulf me. I'm going to drown.

In unison, both of them pull out of me.

I try and chase Dennox's cock with my mouth, and he leans down to kiss me instead. "Wha—?" I protest when his lips leave mine.

"Not yet, *diya*."

"First, we must prepare you to take us," Vulrux adds.

I'm confused until he props my hips higher. My ass waves in the air. I know what's coming.

Sure enough, Vulrux's slick fingers delve between my upturned cheeks. "We will go slowly," he promises. "I will be gentle."

I bite my lip. I know they won't hurt me, but I'm still a little nervous. "Relax," he soothes once again.

Dennox strokes my back, the touch gentle and calming, and I take a deep breath. "Okay, I'm ready."

Vulrux stretches me, first with one, and then two fingers. When he adds the third, I feel a surge of slick wet heat and a moan escapes my lips. "Good?" Vulrux asks, his eyebrow raised.

"Mmm."

Dennox lies down next to me, distracting me with kisses. It works until Vulrux fits a fourth finger into me and pumps slowly.

"Oooooh." "Relax, sweet one." He pulls his fingers out and positions me over his lap. He holds me tight, comforting me as he eases inside. I feel my muscles stretch to accommodate his thickness, and I tense up automatically and clench my hands into fists, but Vulrux is patient. He moves slowly and steadily, and allows me to get used to him before pushing deeper. When he's finally done, I'm seated fully on his cock, my anal muscles rippling around him, stirring up a deep, dark pleasure.

"Good?" Vulrux asks.

"Y-yes."

He rewards me by sucking on my neck. When this is over, I'm going to have some serious Draekon hickeys.

Awesome.

Vulrux moves a little, letting me get comfortable to the sensation of him in my ass. It's definitely strange but in a good way. I feel full and empty at the same time. My pussy muscles flutter, ready for more.

"My turn," Dennox says, his eyes blazing with heat.

Sounds good to me. I spread my legs wider, and he smiles at my invitation. Vulrux lies back, and Dennox kneels in front of me, splaying his palm over my chest and pushing me back until I'm lying flush on top of Vulrux.

"There is something you should know," Dennox says, toying with my breasts, leaning forward to swirl his tongue around my nipples. Total boob draekon.

"What?" I pant.

Dennox bites my breasts lightly, holding my eyes as he scrapes his teeth along my sensitive flesh.

"Vulrux is patient," he says, swinging into position over me. His cock brushes my pussy, and my hips strain upward for more. "I am not."

His giant body settles over me, his biceps bulging by my head as he holds himself up. Reaching down, he fits himself into me. Pinning me with his gaze, he slides inside, inch by inch, centimeter by centimeter, until my inner walls are throbbing, my holes completely stretched.

This is incredible.

"Brace her," Dennox says to Vulrux, who tightens his arms around me as the soldier's hips begin to piston. A flush spreads over me, warmth from deep within, pleasure consuming me. Dennox speeds up until he's fucking me so hard I'm about to fly apart. My breath comes in gasps, my body undulates between the two men. I'm drowning in desire, completely overwhelmed with sensation.

"Don't stop." I hook my hands on Dennox's pumping torso, digging my nails and hanging on for dear life. The move makes him pound harder, and I cry out encouragement. I might die from this pleasure, but if he stops, I definitely won't survive. Each thrust makes me come undone.

"*Diya,*" Vulrux gasps. His hips slam up, his cock pulsing inside me. I cry out as I shatter, a thousand shining droplets of pleasure raining down on me. With a snarl, Dennox plows forward once, twice, and lets out a fierce shout of triumph before he collapses on me. He still holds most of his weight, but he presses his face to my breasts, rubbing his stubble against them before resting his head between them, eyes closed. His expression radiates contentment.

Weak with pleasure, I raise a hand and brush back his dark hair. We lay like that for a few long moments, the silence punctured only by our breathing and the steady dull drumbeats of the downpour outside.

Finally, Dennox stirs, blinking and rising off me. Vulrux sits up and lifts me off his cock. I groan, belly fluttering with aftershocks, my muscles quivering and clenching.

"Wow," I say softly, grinning at my two men. It takes me two tries, but I finally sit up.

Dennox opens his mouth to says something, and a shudder rocks through his giant body. Eyes wide, his head snaps to Vulrux, who frowns. A second later, the light-haired man's body shudders the same way.

In a blur, they both push away from the bed.

"Guys? You okay?"

"Outside," Dennox gasps, pulling at Vulrux.

I roll to my feet, grabbing my clothes and following them as they stumble through the house. I'm not exactly sure what's happening, but I can guess.

They're transforming into dragons.

14

Vulrux:

The air stills as the transformation begins.

Pain fills my body. Near me, Dennox's hands clench into fists, his expression agonized. My nails start to lengthen into claws, and I stare at them blankly. My mind is still hazy with pleasure, my body still sated and lax.

Dennox, with his soldier's quickness, understands what's happening before I do. "The transformation is upon us," he gasps, his face contorted as his bones twist and reshape. "We must go outside."

Bast! Of course. My house is many things, but dragon-proof it's not. The mating bond took longer between Viola, Arax, and Nyx, but Viola hadn't had Draekon blood flowing through her veins. Harper has, and the presence of the mutation must have accelerated the bonding.

Dennox hurtles through the house, and I follow on his heels.

"Harper, stay back!" I shout, and feel relief when she

stops in the doorway, face stricken with worry. I don't have time to tell her what's happening. The dragon is upon me.

The driving rain hammers at my body as I sink to my knees, gasping in agony.

My skin tears. My bones break and reform. For an instant, I can't breathe, and then I feel wings erupt. My skin hardens into scales, and my tail lashes to and fro.

For sixty years, the dragon inside me has waited for this moment. Now, it is free at last.

I rear up and breathe flames into the sky, bellowing my joy at the long-delayed transformation. At my side, a gleaming bronze dragon spreads its wings and arches upward. *Dennox.*

Alerted by my roar, people fill the clearing. My cousin Arax, and his pair-bond, Nyx. Rorix. Ferix. Thrax. Haldax. Their eyes widen with awe as they see the two dragons in front of them.

The rain hammers down, brutal and unrelenting. I snarl my defiance. *I will fly today.* I spread my wings, that glitter blue-green like the color of the underground lake, the color of Harper's eyes.

Pain engulfs me once more as the rain shreds my wings.

Harper's running toward me, as are the others. "Change back," she screams. "Get to the safety of the paths."

I try to yell at her not to stay where she is. To my everlasting gratitude, Nyx grabs her before she runs into the rain. *Thank Caeron.* I take a deep breath. My body seems to know how to transform by instinct because I don't have to think about what to do to become a man again.

We crawl back to the paths. My arms are bruised, battered and sore, but I'm not badly injured; the rain didn't have too much time to do damage.

Harper sinks to her knees beside us, her fingers running over our arms. "Are you okay?"

Dennox nods. "Just cuts and scratches," he says, with a hardiness borne of long years of training. "It'll heal by the morning."

Harper slowly realizes that a hush has fallen over the camp, and every single person is watching us. Including the two scientists. Her cheeks go pink as she takes in the audience. The mating bond causes the transformation; every single Draekon knows that. We might as well have announced that we just had sex.

For a moment, she seems almost speechless, then she shrugs faintly, and her face splits into a broad grin. "Not to be a prude or anything," she quips, "but I really think the two of you should put some clothes on."

Harper:

Holy fucking tamales. They're dragons. Call me superficial, but that's totally, *absolutely* hot.

Dennox's dragon is bronze and powerful. Vulrux's dragon is bluish-green and looks sleek and fast.

And the fire-breathing? Is. So. Cool.

I can't wait to jump them again.

THE OTHER DRAEKONS crowd around my mates—and yes, I guess I'm calling them that—congratulating them, patting them on the back. Ryanna grins at me. "Let me guess, you couldn't resist the hotties," she says, under the chatter.

I laugh. "I guess not." I give her an appraising look. "Which leaves Sofia and you as the single ones."

She rolls her eyes. "Oh God, tell me you're not going to become one of those people," she says. "Everyone doesn't have to be a couple, you know. Or a trio. Some of us are happy being single."

I've watched Ryanna in camp. She totally has a crush on Thrax, and both Thrax and Zorux, have spent hours with her, patiently teaching her how to throw the bone knives they use to hunt.

Of course, neither men transformed into dragons when they laid eyes on her. Maybe that's what's holding her back?

"If you say so," I reply, holding up my hands. "No match-making, I promise."

Viola comes up to me. "Don't say 'I told you so,'" I warn her. "Gloating is a bad look on you."

She doesn't crack a smile. "Can I talk to you alone?" she asks, taking hold of my elbow and leading me away from everyone. When we're out of earshot, she looks at me with a serious expression on her face. "I heard you went to visit Raiht'vi," she says.

So much for Nyx being cool about me visiting the scientist.

"Yeah, is that against the rules?"

She frowns. "Don't be flippant, Harper." She looks around and moves closer. "I don't trust her."

"Why not? She's not exactly winning prizes in the charm department, I grant you that, but she's not that bad."

She takes a deep breath. "I've never told anyone this," she warns. "Not even Arax and Nyx. When you were uncon-scious, Arax and Nyx went to back to the spaceship to get our luggage, which sounds harmless, but wasn't really, because the rains were imminent, and they hadn't transformed."

After seeing what the rains did to my two dragons, I can see why that would be dangerous.

"They wanted it to be a surprise," she continues in a low voice. "When I couldn't find them, Raiht'vi told me that they went to look for the Draekons that took Olivia and the others."

"What?"

She nods grimly. "She was ill," she admits. "And she might have been delirious."

"But you don't believe that."

"No." She gives me a steady look. "I think she said that because she knew I'd go looking for Arax and Nyx in the jungle. I think she was trying to get me killed."

I give her a shocked look. "Are you sure?"

She shakes her head. "No, I'm not. But I don't trust her, Harper. I don't trust either of them. Be careful, okay?"

She turns around and goes back to the others. I stare at her receding back. I know I need to tell Viola about what Vulrux learned from Beirax. I need to tell Ryanna and Sofia too. Even if there's only a slim chance that there's a way out of this planet, the women deserve to know.

"I should tell Arax about what I learned from Beirax."

The three of us are back in the underground lake the next day. As usual, it's deserted, though I have a sneaking suspicion that the privacy is Arax's doing, a way of encouraging the mating bond, and if so, *thank you, Firstborn.*

Dennox was right; yesterday's rain-induced bruises are gone, and both men appear to be in perfect health.

The red *narmi* that scared the crap out of me the first day circles us, but I'm used to seeing it around, and I barely spare it a second glance. Instead, I look at Vulrux. He's floating on his back, the *narmi* playfully butting him every five seconds or so.

"You haven't told him? I thought that's the first thing you'd do."

"No, of course not, Harper," he responds. "I wouldn't have told him before I told you. You're our mate. You always come first."

I can't help the smile that breaks out on my face. Seriously, I'm pinching myself this morning; I feel so lucky. Maybe that's the effect of really good sex.

"Why haven't you told him?" I ask Vulrux.

He has a pensive look on his face. "You didn't know Arax's life on Zoraht," he replies. "From the moment he woke up to the moment he went to bed, his life was dictated for him. In the last year before the Exile, assassins targeted him three times. Palace intrigues, spies, secrets..." He sighs. "It's not easy being the Firstborn."

Dennox raises an eyebrow. "Not just the Firstborn," he points out. "You were causing quite a stir yourself with your speeches in the Saaric."

I find every description of Zoraht fascinating. Even the politics. "What kind of speeches?"

Vulrux shrugs. "The scientists wanted to expand their security force," he says. "Among other things. I spoke out against it. Brunox, the head of their council, is a dangerous man, canny and power-hungry, and he had far too many allies." His face darkens. "Including the Adrashian techmages."

"You think Arax will worry about what's happening on Zoraht."

He nods. "My cousin is finally happy," he says softly.

"Nyx and Viola are really good for him. I've never seen him more relaxed, more content. I don't want to ruin that."

I gaze at the troubled man. "You can't keep this from him though."

"I know," he replies. "I don't plan to. Before the rains end, I will tell him everything." His expression lightens. "In the meanwhile," he says, "I just realized this cave is large enough for us to transform, and even fly."

I look around the vast space. "You can't fly much," I point out. "More like hover." I frown. "You should take it easy after yesterday's injuries."

He grins playfully. "I'll take it just as easy as you did once you woke up from your coma, Harper," he says with a wink.

Ouch.

Dennox's lips twitch. "We should find out what our abilities are," he says practically. "Otherwise, we won't be much use when we look for the other humans."

My eyes sparkle and I smile gleefully. "So the two of you are going to transform again? Yes, please. And are you going to breathe fire too? So cool."

Dennox chuckles at me. He swims to the bank and pulls himself out of the water. Once again, I ogle shamelessly as the water sluices off him, and all that glorious nakedness comes into view. Yum. And it's mine.

He takes a deep breath. I watch, transfixed, as he morphs into a dragon. I swear, if I live to be a hundred years old, I'm never going to get tired of the sight.

Vulrux gets up from his rocky perch and joins me. "Can you understand us?" he yells to dragon-Dennox. "Can you recognize us?"

Dragon-Dennox's long neck curls toward us, and the massive head nods slowly.

Well, that's a relief.

Vulrux keeps asking questions. "Can you hover?" he yells to Dennox.

The bronze dragon makes his way to the rock that Vulrux was sitting on, his tail slithering behind him. *He's using the rock formation as a launch pad,* I realize. I watch as dragon-Dennox climbs the rocks, oddly graceful and cat-like. When he reaches the top, he unfurls his wings, jumps, and swoops low over the lake.

It lasts for about five seconds before he runs out of room and splashes into the water.

Most awesome five seconds ever.

Vulrux is almost bent over with laughter. Dragon-Dennox slithers out of the water. He shifts back and heads over, his eyes narrowed as he takes in the other man's amusement. "Really?" he demands. "This is funny to you? You're doing the next set of experiments."

"Oh, come on." I wrap my hand around Dennox's waist. "That was hilarious."

He tries to glare at me, but he can't pull it off. His lips twitch, and finally, he too bursts out laughing.

Vulrux transforms next. "Let's try breathing fire," Dennox suggests to the blue-green dragon. "Can you burn that bush on the far side of the lake?"

The dragon opens his mouth and exhales a jet of fire. The bush bursts into flame and dragon-Vulrux looks smug.

I bounce on the balls of my feet and clap loudly. Dennox, on the other hand, has a frown on his face. "Did it just get colder here?"

He's right. Now that he mentions it, I'm suddenly freezing, and when I look at the rocks, they're covered with a thin sheen of ice.

"Try again," Dennox shouts to Vulrux. "Aim anywhere."

Vulrux opens his mouth, but this time around, only a

wisp of fire leaks out before being extinguished. He shifts back. "That's strange. What's happening?"

Dennox's brow clears. "You're drawing heat from the air to create fire," he says. "The temperature dropped when you burned the bush. I bet," he adds, "that you'll be fine once it warms up again. Or if you move to a different area."

Vulrux looks thoughtful. "That is a liability."

"Is it?" I ask quizzically. "I'm assuming you only need one burst of fire to do damage."

Vulrux's lips turn up. "You're probably right." His fingertips run over the swell of my breasts. "I don't know," he murmurs, "Why I'm exploring my new found abilities when I could be doing something much more interesting."

Dennox's hand moves down my back, and he cups my butt. "Mmm," he growls. "I agree with Vulrux." He fixes me with a heated gaze. "Why are you wearing your swimsuit today, *diya?*"

I roll my eyes. "Because I wanted to swim," I reply. "If I were naked, I'm pretty sure none of us would have got into the water."

Vulrux tugs at the shoulder-straps of my suit. "You swam already," he says. "And now, the garment is just in the way." He undresses me, pressing kisses on my heated skin.

"I have a confession..."

"Yes?" Dennox pulls me to him and lifts me in his arms. I wrap my arms and legs around him as he walks me back to the smooth rocks where we fooled around before.

"The fact that you guys are dragons is a major turn on," I admit.

"Turn on? What are you telling us, Harper?" the mischievous glint in his eye says he knows exactly what I'm hinting at.

I push at him. "Why would I tell you when I can show

you?" I wriggle out of his arms, sliding down his naked body, tugging him to sit. I kneel before him and grip his cock again. "This time is all about you," I tell him. He doesn't protest. Smart draekon.

"You too." I beckon to Vulrux.

He joins the two of us, wrapping his hand around my neck and turning me toward him. I taste one cock and then the other, marveling at the rich honey taste. "This is incredible," I mutter.

"Does it taste good?" Vulrux asks.

"Yes. Like honey. Something sweet."

As I suck them, they play with my nipples, pinching them and pulling them. My breasts go heavy with desire, and I gasp with pleasure at their touch. "So incredible..." *Gotta love dragons.* A thought strikes me. "Do you think I could ride on your back sometime? In dragon form?"

"We must make sure you are safe—" Vulrux starts, and I wrap my mouth around the head of his cock and suck lightly. His fingers fist in my hair, but I pull off with a pop.

"What was that again, Vulrux?"

The gleam in his eyes tells me he knows exactly what I'm doing. Before he can answer, I take a deep breath and engulf him as far as I can. His knees almost buckle, and he groans audibly. I work my mouth over him, sucking until my cheeks hollow. As soon as I relax the suction, he stumbles back, chest heaving.

Dennox chuckles as if he knows my game. I turn to him. "What do you think, Dennox?" I purr. "Can I ride you?"

"I don't know, *diya*. Can you?" He leans back, his cock sticking straight up. Clearly, he wants me to ride him in this form. Normally I would hop right on, but today I want to blow his mind.

Nestling between his knees, I lick his balls and then

scoot forward to wrap my boobs around his dick. His eyes widen as I squeeze his shaft between his two favorite things. "Like this?" I breathe, and bob up and down, sliding my breasts along his slick cock. On the down stroke, I bend my head to close my lips over his head.

Dennox's hips jerk. "Harper," he says through gritted teeth.

"Is that a yes?" I say, and stroke faster, sucking harder until he roars and thrusts his hips up high. "Mouth," he grunts, his face contorted with desire. Obligingly, I take him in my mouth again. He's close. His hand on the back of my head holding me close, he comes deep in my throat, and I swallow every drop.

"Harper Boyd," Dennox gasps.

"Yes?" I ask, giving him my most innocent smile.

The dark-haired Draekon just shakes his head.

"You've robbed him of words, sweet one," Vulrux says. He lifts me from my knees and smooths back my hair.

I smile up at him. "It's your turn." I close my palm over Vulrux's fat cock, marveling once again at how thick and hard he is. My fist slides up and down his length, and he throws his head back in pleasure.

Dennox pulls me into his lap. He spreads my legs wide, and moves his fingers between my legs, unerringly finding my clitoris and strumming on it. Groaning with pleasure, I reach for Vulrux, and take his cock in my mouth, savoring the sweet taste of him. We're both pretty close.

His fingers increase their pressure on my clitoris, and I moan into Vulrux's cock. I'm so close, but I fight to hold on. My Draekons have given me endless pleasure. Today, I want it to be about them. I want Vulrux to come first.

Vulrux's grip tightens in my hair. His normal control unravels, and he thrusts into my mouth. *I did this to him.*

"Diya," he gasps, his voice hoarse. Then he erupts, and I swallow every drop. Dennox's fingers speed up, and I can't hold back anymore. A dam bursts, and wave after wave of sweet release flows through me.

When it's done, I lick my lips. Honey and cream. Delicious.

"Dragons are awesome."

15

Harper:

A couple of days go by, and life falls into a kind of rhythm. Every morning, after breakfast, we go swimming. After that, we each head off to our tasks. Vulrux makes salves, tinctures, and ointments out of the medicinal herbs he's gathered during the dry season, and when he's not doing that, he's in charge of making *kunnr* wine.

Dennox carves bone knives and mends the pathways, which always appear in need of repair.

Me? I've been assigned the laborious task of weaving the tree bark together so we can use it as roofing. I should find the work mind-numbingly boring, but as I fiddle with the fibers, I feel myself relaxing for the first time in a long time.

It's a peaceful life on the prison planet. One with friends and laughter, food and drink, warmth and happiness. One with love. There's a community here that I never had back home and a sense of belonging.

Sometimes, I think of the cloakship that Beirax

mentioned, but the urge to find it is never very strong. Once the rains stop, I know we'll go looking for it, but I can't say I'm in a huge hurry for things to change.

The truth is, things are pretty damn good as they are.

SOFIA and I are preparing the evening meal for the first time, and we're running terribly, horribly behind. "Dios Mio," she groans. "Ferix asked me if we needed help and I told him we had it under control."

Newsflash: She was lying.

"Yeah," I mutter. "I know. I was there."

Vulrux and Dennox are in the dining area as well, watching with open amusement. Dennox comes over to the small prep area, where Sofia and I are trying to dance around each other. "Are you sure we can't help you, Harper?" he asks, his eyes twinkling with mirth. "The two of you seem to be having some trouble."

"Men," Sofia says under her breath.

"Stop laughing at us," I tell Dennox sternly. "I'll have you know that back on Earth, I was an excellent cook." Okay, I might be exaggerating just a little bit. "On Earth though, we had electric stoves and microwaves and meat thermometers."

The translator in his ear does its magic. Dennox encircles me from behind and kisses the side of my neck. "Poor Harper," he whispers in my ear, his voice still amused. "How ever are you going to manage?"

Sofia rolls her eyes. "Can the three of you make out later?" she demands. "Harper, the others are going to be here for dinner *any minute now*, and all we have is burnt meat and mush. Get peeling."

Dennox winks at me and leaves us alone. He joins

Vulrux, and the two of them are soon in deep conversation. If I had to guess what they're talking about, it's Beirax's revelations and Dennox's memories. This morning, Vulrux decided to tell Arax everything after the evening meal.

All the more reason why Sofia and I need to hurry up and get food on the table.

I get to work on peeling knotty purple roots in front of me. Sofia, who's much better at names than I am, told me what plant it came from, but I've forgotten already. As far as I'm concerned, the only thing that matters is that the roots taste a little like turnip. Ugh.

"Be careful with that bone knife," Sofia warns me as she tears some pink leaves and throws them into a clay pot along with the few pieces of meat she's been able to salvage from our earlier barbeque debacle. "It's a lot sharper than it looks."

"Yes mother," I quip.

We work in silence for a few moments, and I shoot Dennox and Vulrux several covert looks. When I'm certain they're not paying attention to me, I clear my throat. "Hey, Sofia, there's something I've been meaning to ask you."

She doesn't lift her head from the pot. "Uh-huh," she says. "What's up?"

"Umm, this is a little awkward. I kinda heard that you and Vulrux might have had a thing for each other when I was in a coma."

That gets her attention. She gives me a stupefied look. "What?"

I bite my lower lip. "If you don't want to talk about it..." My voice trails off.

She continues to gape at me. "Harper," she says at last, "I've never had a thing for Vulrux. From the moment you got here, Vulrux couldn't take his eyes off you."

Oh. I'm going to kill Viola. She might have got the Thrax-Ryanna thing right, but she missed the boat entirely on this one. "Are you sure?" I ask her.

"I'm quite sure," she replies dryly. "You're welcome to your Draekons, Harper. I'm not pining for either of them. Now, can you get peeling, please? I'm pretty sure I just saw Strax and Odix walk toward the dining area."

Crap. She's right. It's not just the two Draekons, I see a stream of people heading toward us, and we don't have anything for them to eat. I'm about to start peeling faster when I see someone unexpected walking our way.

It's Raiht'vi.

The Zorahn scientist has finally decided to join us for a meal.

THERE'S a bit of awkward shuffling at first, but then Haldax, who never met a Highborn he didn't love, starts talking to Raiht'vi. Viola watches the scientist with narrowed eyes, and I remember our conversation from the other day. Did Raiht'vi send Viola into the jungle, knowing how dangerous it would be? Or was it all a big misunderstanding?

I can't tell. The scientist is too inscrutable.

Someone else is watching Raiht'vi. Dennox. My mate's expression is uncertain, and his shoulders are tense.

After her initial look of surprise, Sofia's returned to her cooking, moving at a frantic pace. I don't see what the big deal is—so what if dinner's a little late anyway? It's our first time alone in the kitchen. While I want to impress Vulrux and Dennox, I'm not going to twist myself into knots about my culinary abilities.

Sofia isn't quite as calm. The instant I'm done peeling

and chopping the purple turnip-thingamabobs, she snatches the wooden cutting board from me.

It seems to happen in slow motion.

The bone knife that I'd set down next to the roots goes flying in the air. Acting instinctively, I make a grab for it, but my fingers don't close around the handle.

They close around the razor-sharp blade.

I stare at my hand. A thin red line appears, blood trickling down my wrist. *It's nothing serious,* I tell myself, and then the flow increases. Blood begins to seep from the cut, slowly but steadily, dripping on the floor.

The knife clatters to the ground, and the noise makes Vulrux and Dennox look up. The instant they see my face, they're at my side. Dennox makes a strangled noise in his throat and goes pale.

Vulrux swallows hard. "How deep?" he asks, his voice shaky. "Flex your fingers for me, *diya*."

"It's just a cut," I say, but I'm beginning to feel light-headed from the blood loss. I lean on my two mates, grateful for their support. "It's nothing serious. I'm not going to be a juggler anytime soon though."

Before either of them have a chance to respond, Raiht'vi comes up. "Let me see," she orders. I obediently show her my hand, and she surveys it for a few seconds and then shrugs dismissively. "It's a minor cut," she says. "It won't hurt you. The wound will heal."

It's a good thing Raiht'vi never became a doctor because her bedside manner sucks ass.

Dennox's fingers dig into my flesh, jerking my attention to my mate. His face has gone even whiter, and he's staring at Raiht'vi in horror. "I remember you," he says. "You were in the Crimson Citadel. You were one of the people that experimented on me."

He takes a deep breath, and when he speaks next, there's a note of raw anger in his voice, one I've never heard from him. "You were there that night, working late. Everyone else had left. *I remember.*"

A stillness spreads over the crowd. Arax stalks over. "What are you saying, Dennox?" he asks, his voice soft and filled with menace.

Dennox is still looking at Raiht'vi. "I remember the guards coming in with the news that Vulrux was in the citadel. You asked them if any of the more senior scientists were around, but nobody was there except you." His eyes haze with pain. "Did you..."

Raiht'vi straightens to her full, impressive height. Her face is set in hard lines. "Yes," she says. "I did. I gave the order that killed your mate."

Dennox breaks from his stillness, lunging towards Raiht'vi, who does not recoil. She stands bravely as the warrior charges. Shouts rise from everyone. "Dennox, stop," Arax orders. "No," I cry out, adding my voice to the mix, but he cannot hear me.

"You," Dennox roars, "You will not hurt our mate!"

A body blurs past Raiht'vi, slamming into Dennox. It's Thrax, trying to stop my warrior mate. The blow forces him back, but in a smooth move, Dennox ducks and sends the leaner alien flying, crashing into the staring crowd. Thrax springs back to his feet, shakes his head and rushes back, but he's no match for Dennox, who moves with the skill and speed of an elite soldier.

Nyx rushes Dennox, feinting at the last moment to slip past his defenses. The two Draekons wrestle, Thrax jumping on the pile, grabbing Dennox's arm as he slams Nyx to the floor. More Draekons rush to help.

Cool air washes over my skin, a shocking change from

the broiling humidity. My skin prickles with the significance.

Dennox is calling his dragon.

"No," I scream louder, and start pushing through the crowd, trying to get to him.

Vulrux whirls and catches me, lifting me into his arms. "We must get you to safety." There's fear in his voice. He's realized what I have: Dennox is no longer in control.

"Dennox, please," I sob, terror washing over me. Somehow, my voice catches my warrior mate's ear in the chaos and the tumult.

"Harper?" He turns to find me, almost pulling Nyx and two others off their feet. My heart breaks at the confusion in his eyes. He seems to slowly gather his wits. He draws in a deep breath and takes a half-step toward me.

"Yes, that's it," Vulrux breathes. "He's back in control."

Nyx and Thrax get a hold of Dennox's arms, but he's no longer fighting. He looks straight at me, his chest rising and falling like he's run a marathon. "I'm sorry," he whispers. "I snapped."

"Almost," I correct him. "You didn't, though. What happened?"

"He remembers," Vulrux murmurs, and I realize why Dennox charged Raiht'vi. For a moment Dennox was back in that awful place, watching his first mate die, helpless to protect her. His instincts kicked in when he remembered what Raiht'vi had done.

"She killed your mate," I whisper, feeling ill.

"She gave the order," Vulrux says quietly. His mouth is twisted, and his eyes are filled with pain. My heart aches at the sight. I want to cling to him, but he steps away, towards Dennox, and I let him go.

"Enough," Arax says. He has his arms around Viola,

shielding her from any possible danger. A motion from him, and Nyx and Thrax release Dennox. The Firstborn gives Raiht'vi a long, assessing stare. The scientist's face is pale, but she still stands tall. "I will see the affected parties in my house," Arax says icily. He glances around at us. "Vulrux and Dennox. This crime was committed on the homeworld. By the laws of Zoraht, you, as the injured party, may pass judgment on Raiht'vi. You will decide," he pauses and draws in a deep breath, "whether she lives or dies."

Vulrux and Dennox are looking at Raiht'vi in stunned horror.

I want to be sick. All the while, I've been trying to convince myself that the two men aren't still broken up by the death of their mate, ignoring the signs that pointed otherwise. I've tried to forget that the real reason Vulrux drugged Beirax is because he wanted to know the truth of that night. I've turned a blind eye to the fact that Dennox didn't want to mate with me until his memories reappeared.

I'm a fool. A stupid, love-struck fool wearing rose-tinted glasses.

It's clear from their expressions that Vulrux and Dennox never got over their first mate. *And I don't know where that leaves me.*

16

Dennox:

For the last few days, I was happier than I'd ever been in my life. Harper's quick wit, her ready smiles, the clear bell-like notes of her laugh filled my heart and soothed my soul, and I was truly content.

Then Raiht'vi tells Harper her wound will heal, and when I hear those words, the veil obscuring my memories is ripped away. Images crash over me in a tidal wave, and I remember everything.

Arriving in the Crimson Citadel. Disarming the guards during an unattended moment, and making a break for it, only to be brought down at the gates by a battalion of Brunox's guards.

The first few months, the scientists that experimented on me were interested in my powers of healing. Sharp knives would slice into me in precise strokes, and the indigo-clad men and women would stand around and watch me bleed, noting my pain responses and measuring the precise moment when my wounds began to knit.

Then they brought the woman in and tried to unravel the mysteries of the Draekon mating bond.

I remember when Raiht'vi first arrived at the underground labs. Her eyes had widened with horror and pity when she'd seen the two of us, bound on examination tables. She'd realized at once that she was witnessing an act of treason. By kidnapping a Zoraken, the scientists were declaring war on the High Emperor.

I remember her body trembling with fear as she was told what she would have to do. She'd been young then, a little over fifteen, a third-year apprentice with immense talent, but with a fatal flaw. She'd had a conscience.

I watched as the senior scientists stripped that away from her, the same way they stripped away my freedom, my pride and my sense of dignity. So many times in the underground citadel, I'd wanted to kill myself, to end the pain and the horror of what I'd stumbled into.

Then one night, Vulrux had appeared, and everything had changed.

At my side, Harper's stiff and pale. I put my arm around her shoulder, taking comfort in her softness, breathing in her warmth. I'm profoundly grateful that we were lucky enough to find her. "I need you, *diya*," I say quietly into her ear. "Come with us."

She doesn't respond but lost as I am in my thoughts, I don't notice.

∽

Vulrux:

So many conflicting emotions.

I don't know what to think. My entire world has been

upended. My emotions swirl over me like an angry sea, and I'm afraid I'm going to drown under the weight of my past.

But at my side, there's a woman that anchors me to the present. In my past, there is darkness, but Harper Boyd is my present and my future. A woman who has brought color and laughter back into my world, a woman who makes me want to *live*, not just survive.

"I don't get it," I'd told Arax once, shortly after Viola came to the camp and Arax introduced her as his mate. "I don't understand how you can take one look at a stranger from a faraway planet, and know that you belong together. Isn't it important that you get to know a woman and find out if there's something deeper than sexual attraction that binds you together?"

He'd looked at me, a typically serious expression on his face. "My soul recognizes Viola," he'd said. "I don't know how to explain it, Vulrux. What I feel for her is so much more than a physical urge. Until she arrived in my life, I didn't know that there was a hole in it, but now that she's here, I can't imagine my life without her."

I think of my cousin's words now. Sixty years ago, the dragon inside me recognized the woman in the underground lab as my mate, but she'd been killed before I could even say a word to her.

It's so much better with Harper. The dragon inside me wants her, but that urge is primal. The dragon doesn't appreciate the sparkle in her eyes, but I do. The dragon doesn't see the way her gaze softens when she looks at Dennox and me, but I do. The dragon doesn't value her sharp wit and keen curiosity, but I do.

Harper is more than our mate. She's the woman I'm in love with.

Without Raiht'vi's intervention, our first mate would still be alive.

Without Raiht'vi's intervention, Harper would have died.

THE SEVEN OF us crowd into Arax's living space. Viola's eyes are wide and worried. Nyx's usual cheerful expression has been replaced by a grim sternness. Harper is pale and quiet. "Is your hand hurting you?" I murmur.

"No," she whispers back. Her tone is uncharacteristically flat, sending a pinprick of worry down my spine.

Once upon a time, I would have sworn that I wanted revenge on the person that took my mate away from me. Now, the need for vengeance is dimmed. I'm too aware that if it hadn't been for Raiht'vi, Harper would be dead.

One life taken. One life saved.

Arax is about to open his mouth, but before he does, I lift my hand to forestall him. "Before we do this," I say to my cousin, "I need to tell you something." I glance at the Zorahn scientist, whose expression is unreadable. "Privately."

The urgency of my tone isn't lost on the room. "I'll escort Raiht'vi back to Zorux's house," Nyx says. "And arrange for a guard."

Raiht'vi chuckles bitterly. "A guard? Where am I going to go, Thief? The rains trap me on this mountain."

"Nonetheless," Arax replies, his voice harsh. "I refuse to take any chances."

When Nyx returns, I take a deep breath. "For years," I begin, "it's eaten away at me that that woman was killed because of me."

"Because of both of us," Dennox interjects. "This isn't your fault alone."

I nod to my pair-bond. "Had we not transformed inside the Crimson Citadel, she would still be alive. Many nights, I've stayed awake, consumed with guilt that I was responsible for her death."

"*We* were responsible for her death," Dennox mutters under his breath. "Not just you."

Arax agrees with the soldier. "You are Draekon," he says. "You cannot control the first transformation. The person responsible for the death of your mate," he says, "is the person that gave the order for her to be killed."

I ignore the interruption and get to the point. "When the scientists crashed on the prison planet, I burned to know the truth. I questioned Beirax."

"How?" Nyx asks. "Arax couldn't get the man to talk."

My cheeks flush. "*Ahuma* venom is a very effective truth serum. In the last sixty years, I've managed to collect two vials of it. I used one on Beirax."

Nyx whistles under his breath and Arax surveys me with an astonished expression on his face. "You drugged a patient, violating the core principles of your training as a healer? It mattered that much that you knew?"

It did, but not for the reasons he believes. Dennox was resolute that he wouldn't complete the mating bond until he knew what his missing memories concealed. My motivations were more complex. For sixty years, I was obsessed with discovering the truth. I had to find out, if only to lay my long quest to rest and focus on the future.

"It's complicated," I murmur. "Besides, I never completed my training as a healer. I didn't take the final oaths."

Nyx's eyes flicker to Harper, and then back to me. I understand the unspoken message. The thief has an unerring ability to hone in on what's truly important, and he's right. My past lies behind me. A future with Harper lies ahead.

My mate seems distressed, her face pale and pinched with misery. I wonder if it is because she thinks we're going to demand that Raiht'vi be killed for her crimes. I want to reassure her and tell her that I have no such bloodlust, but first, I need to tell Arax what I discovered.

"What did you learn from Beirax?"

"His purpose was to learn if the human women could mate with us," I reply. "But that's not the most important thing." I draw a deep breath. "Beirax claims that the Order of the Crimson Night has been dropping supplies on the prison planet, and somewhere out there," I wave a hand to the jungle below us, "there are the component parts of a Cloakship, waiting to be assembled. Beirax never intended to be exiled on the prison planet. He had a way back home."

Arax's head snaps up with shock. Even Nyx looks intrigued. "What's a Cloakship?" Viola asks.

"A top-of-the-line spaceship," Arax replies grimly. "Small, faster than light, and virtually undetectable. Only one planet in the known universe possesses the ability to make them."

Understanding dawns in Dennox's eyes. "Adrash. Of course. That's why we were sent into battle. The High Emperor wanted to bring the techmages under his control."

The Firstborn's eyes narrow. "How did you know about Adrash?"

"I fought in that battle," he replies. "I watched soldiers die around me." His lips twist into a bitter smile. "At least now, I know why."

A cold realization cuts through me. "You were captured by techmages," I say slowly, looking at my pair-bond. "Who surrendered you to the scientists." My mind spins as I try and understand what's going on. "Why would the scientists ally themselves with an enemy of the High Emperor?"

Arax's voice is cold. "Brunox covets power," he says. "I advised my father to take precautions, but he liked the man, and he wouldn't listen to me. Then I was exiled."

The four of us go around in circles for many minutes, trying to figure out the ramifications of everything we've learned. Finally, Viola cuts in. "Guys," she says. "Do you know where Harper went?"

Just as she speaks, a great wave of unease washes over me. Our mate is in trouble. I can feel it.

17

Harper:

I can't compete with a ghost.

I'm standing in Arax's living area, listening to Dennox and Vulrux talk about the past, and suddenly, I can't take it anymore. I need air and space and quiet, and I need to be alone.

I can't go back to the dining area. Sofia and Ryanna are going to demand answers from me. The Draekons are going to surround me, and everyone's going to be discussing Vulrux and Dennox's dead mate.

I can't go back to Vulrux's house. The three of us have shared a bed for days. Everything in there will remind me of the two men I've fallen in love with.

My eyes fill with tears, and there's a lump in my throat, making it difficult to swallow. *Harper,* I chide, *you're overreacting. This woman has been dead for sixty years, and Dennox and Vulrux never really knew her. You're freaking out about nothing.*

Hope trickles through me. Maybe there's nothing to be worried about.

The lake. That's exactly what I need. Lap after lap in the underground lake, until my muscles are exhausted, and my mind is calmed.

Everyone's still in the dining area, but they're sitting around the table in the outer room, deep in conversation. I move quietly into the inner room, taking care to avoid attracting any attention. I just need to be by myself for a little while.

As silently as I can, I open the trapdoor in the floor. Grabbing one of the lamps in the room, I head down the long flight of stairs.

I'M at the stone archway at the bottom of the stairs when I hear someone behind me. The hair on the back of my neck rises. Before I can turn, there's a sharp knife against my throat.

"Harper Boyd," a harsh voice says. "I've been waiting for this moment."

Beirax.

Fuck.

My heart pounds in my chest. "What are you doing?" I demand. "What's the point of this? Do you think that Vulrux and Dennox aren't going to notice I'm missing? Because they will."

"I'm counting on it," he replies coolly. "Your Draekons are an integral part of my plan."

My palms dampen with fear. "What do you mean? What do you want with them?"

"They can fly," he says. "They're going to take me to my cloakship, stupid human." He pushes me through the archway. "Hold up your lamp. I need to find a spot where the Draekons can't sneak up on me."

He presses the blade against my neck as he speaks. My hand still throbs from the cut earlier this evening, a reminder that bleeding to death will be exceptionally painful and unpleasant. Gritting my teeth, I hold up the lamp.

"That way." He gestures to the formation of rocks that the three of us have been using as a diving board. It's the same spot from which Dennox tried to fly a few days ago. My lips curl into a grin as I remember the short-lived attempt, only to be wiped away when the full meaning of Beirax's words sink in.

"They can't fly in the rain," I say, the pitch of my voice rising in fear. "You saw what happened to their wings."

"So they get hurt." The indifference in his voice stuns me. "They'll heal. Draekons always heal."

I remember the angry-looking welts and bruises on Vulrux and Dennox's arms. *They'd only been in the rain for a few short moments...* My stomach churns with anxiety. I have to think of some way out of this situation. I can't let Beirax use me to force my mates to cooperate.

"You don't know that," I say, trying to reason with the crazy Zorahn. "If they crash mid-flight, you'll die."

"They won't crash." He sounds confident, and a chill seeps through me. This is the same guy who crashed our spaceship on the prison planet. He's a fanatic, intent only on his cause, indifferent to the damage caused by his actions. "They won't crash because you're coming with me, and your precious Draekons will never risk anything happening to you. You think I'm going to let you out of my sight before I'm safely away from this hellhole of a planet? I don't think so, human."

Once upon a time, not too long ago, the idea of escaping the prison planet would have made me dance with glee. Not now, and not like this.

Beirax pushes me on the rocks and positions himself behind me, the knife staying at my throat. "Now we wait," he says. "If I'm right, your Draekons aren't too far behind."

"We're not." There's so much vibrating anger in Vulrux's voice that I barely recognize it. "If you want to live, Beirax, let Harper go right now."

"You're in no position to make threats, Thirdborn," Beirax sneers. "If you want your mate to live, I suggest you do exactly as I say."

18

Dennox:

"Keep him talking. Keep him distracted."

Vulrux nods, his face a mask of tension. I feel the same panic in my heart, but I will myself not to fall to pieces. This is not the time for fear.

I've been a soldier since I hit puberty. My training was brutal, painful, and stunningly effective. I was a commander of the finest fighting machine in the galaxy. I was Zoraken.

Everything that's happened in my life has brought me to this point. Every hour of training, every moment of battle, every enemy vanquished. It was all for this moment. It was so that I could save Harper.

Arax and Nyx have followed us down. Arax places his hand on my arm. "If you can," he says in a low whisper, "take him alive."

I understand why the Firstborn wants Beirax alive. The scientist is a valuable source of information, and I'm sure that Arax wants to question him about the scientists' plans, but I don't care about Zorahn politics.

I just care about Harper.

I make my way silently to the opposite bank of the lake. I've spent hours here, and I know the terrain intimately, which is a blessing because the underground lake is pitch dark. I move silently but swiftly, counting on the noise of the rainfall to muffle my footsteps.

Beirax has positioned himself well. His back is to the rocks, and no one can sneak up behind him without him hearing them first. If I got close to him, I could disarm him easily, but the lake is in the way, and I can't reach them.

I keep an eye on Harper. She's nervous, but she's not panicking. She adds her voice to Vulrux's. "He's right, you know," she says to Beirax. "This is a stupid plan. You'll need to sleep sometime. You'll get tired, hungry, thirsty. My mates are stronger than you. There's no way out."

My mates, she says, without the slightest bit of hesitation in her voice. My heart swells with love when I hear her say those words.

"I'll improvise," Beirax replies, but his tone is uncertain, and I see his grip on the knife waver. Good. Vulrux and Harper are doing their job perfectly. Beirax is starting to get afraid.

If I could fly, I could snatch the man away with my claws, but we've already discovered that the cave isn't large enough for flight.

Which leaves only one way to save our mate. Dragon flame. A narrow burst of fire aimed at the Zorahn scientist, forcing him to drop the knife.

But he's too close to Harper. I cannot risk hurting our mate, and I have only one shot at rescuing her.

We were unable to save one mate; we cannot fail again. Harper is my life, my heart, my future. I must save her.

I get on my knees and force the shift, barely registering

the pain that sweeps through my entire body. Bones break and reform. My skin hardens into scales, and my tail sweeps the ground. My claws pierce the soft soil. *Careful,* the man inside me whispers. *We have only one chance.*

Then I hear it.

Vulrux makes a familiar chirping sound under his breath. *Of course.* The *narmi.* The crimson snake's den is near the cluster of rocks where Beirax is holding a knife to Harper's throat. If it hears Vulrux, if it emerges from the rocks—

My focus sharpens, and I wait. Vulrux chirps again, and this time, I see it. A flicker of movement in the bushes, then the narmi slithers out of its den and makes its way toward Harper, drawn to her familiar presence.

Beirax flinches when he sees the snake. "What is that thing?" he says, backing away in fear.

Now. I open my jaw and exhale fire. My strike finds its target. Beirax shrieks with agony as the hand holding the knife blisters and burns. Screaming, he dives into the lake, dousing the flames that engulf his arm.

"DRAGONS ARE SO COOL." Harper's voice vibrates with excitement as we fold her into our arms. "Calling the narmi was genius. Burning Beirax's hand? Call me bloodthirsty, but that was fantastic. You guys are my heroes."

My lips curve into an amused smile. I want to be mad at Harper for putting her life in danger, but my anger drains away in the face of her obvious enthusiasm.

Vulrux and I wrap our arms around her. "You know," Vulrux says mildly, "you really shouldn't be swimming by yourself in the middle of the night."

"I know," Harper replies. "I just needed to be alone for a bit, that's all."

There's a sudden bleakness in her tone. "*Diya,* what's wrong?" I ask her gently.

She avoids our gaze. "The two of you treat me so well," she whispers. "You're kind to me, you take good care of me. You make me laugh. You protect me."

"Harper." Vulrux puts a finger on her chin and tips her face up. "Why do you sound so sad?"

She swallows. "Because I'll always be second best," she says. "I know it's stupid of me to be jealous of a dead woman. I should be grateful for what I have, not be sick at the thought that you're both still in love with her."

"In love with her?" Vulrux sounds astonished. "What are you talking about, sweet one? There's only one person I'm in love with, and that's you."

"But you interrogated Beirax because you wanted to know who killed your mate."

"I did," he agrees. "I feel responsible for her death. Had we not shifted that day in the Crimson Citadel, she would still be alive. I've burned to identify the person responsible." He draws in a deep breath. "I interrogated Beirax," he says quietly, "Because I wanted to let go of the past. Because I wanted to fully embrace my present and my future." He kisses the palm of her hand softly, careful not to reopen the cut. "My future with you."

I press a kiss on her lips and pick up where Vulrux left off. "I love you, Harper Boyd. I've never felt this way about anyone. You are everything to me."

"Really?"

"I promise."

Her face breaks out into a bright smile, and she hugs us tight. "I love you too," she says, burying her face in our shoulders. Her voice lowers. "And when we go back up to Vulrux's house, I'll show you exactly how much I care about you."

I run my hand over her gentle curves, feeling the warmth of her skin, luxuriating in her sweet softness. My heart swells with happiness. She's ours.

"I heard that," Nyx grumbles. "Fine, the three of you go do your thing. Arax and I will manage Beirax."

"Let them be," Arax advises, his voice amused. "Beirax is in no condition to cause trouble. We'll put a guard on him and a guard on Raiht'vi, and deal with this in the morning. We have problems of our own. Viola's not going to be happy that we forbid her from following us."

Harper snorts with amusement. "Yeah, I can imagine you have some groveling to do," she says. "Hey Arax?" He looks up at our mate, and she flushes. "I was kinda mad at you when you insisted I had to hang out with Vulrux and Dennox."

His expression softens. "And now?"

She smiles at him. "I'm pretty damn happy," she says. "Thanks for that. Maybe you did know what you were doing, after all."

~

Harper:

"Confession," I whisper as Dennox sets me down on the bed. Halfway to the house, he asked if he could carry me, and I couldn't bring myself to say no. Besides, after today, I want to wrap my arms around my mates and never let go. "I love your dragons."

"We know, Harper. And we have decided..."

"Yes?"

Dennox grins at my eagerness. "As soon as the rains stop, we will carry you on our backs as we fly."

Squee!

"As long as it is safe," Vulrux adds.

I roll my eyes at his caution, but Dennox nods agreement. "Vulrux is right, reckless one," he says. "By then you might be pregnant with our child."

"Pregnant?" I test the idea in my head. To my surprise, I don't hate the thought. Huh. I always liked the idea of kids, but after my last horrible relationship with Tom the Terrible, I'd lost faith that I'd ever meet a man who'd I want kids with. Much less two. "Will they be Draekons?"

"Most likely," Vulrux replies. "Though it is impossible to be certain of anything. There is much for us to learn."

I inch to the edge of the bed and clasp my arms around Dennox's neck, kissing him deeply. "What should we do until the rainy season ends?" I ask, my voice innocent.

Dennox's eyes go hooded. "I'm sure we'll think of something." He groans as I slip my hand into his pants and squeeze his cock. Giant, sexy dragon dick. All mine.

Vulrux climbs on the bed behind me. I push back and grind my ass against him while undoing Dennox's pants. His cock jumps out, thick and hard, and I can't resist. Licking my lips, I get on all fours, lowering my mouth on his hard shaft.

Vulrux's fingers tease my clit before he thrusts two fingers into my pussy. I arch my back, trying to press his fingers deeper. His other hand plays with my ass, and I shiver in pleasure. So good. "You're in such a hurry for the rains to end, Harper," he says, his voice rough with lust. "You want to fly, *diya?*" His fingers slide in and out of my pussy, and I whimper into Dennox's cock.

I'm already flying.

Dennox pulls me away from his cock. "I want to be inside you, sweet one," he says. I kiss my way up his chest. Time to play with his nipple rings. The big guy strokes my back, sucking in a breath as I take the metal in my teeth and tug lightly.

Vulrux's thumb brushes over my clitoris before pulling away. "Before we claim her," he says to Dennox, "I want her screaming with pleasure." His strong hands pull me backward. I lose my balance and end up sitting on his chest. Smiling, he lifts me up and positions me so that my pussy hovers over his face. "What do you think, Harper?"

"Sounds good to me," I say with a grin, and lower myself down.

SEVERAL HOURS—OR is it days?—later, I rouse myself from my second coma on this planet.

"I love dragon dick," I rasp. This wasn't how I expected my life to turn out, but I wouldn't change a thing. I'm glad I gave these guys a chance. "And I love you."

Vulrux smiles. He lies on one side of me, his hand threaded in mine. "And we love you, Harper. Mate."

"Mate," Dennox echoes, taking my other hand. Then his expression turns wicked. "I want to taste you now," he says.

Yep. Dream guys. Dream life. Even if it's not quite what I wanted when I came out of my coma—I'm glad I woke up.

"Harper? You ready?"

"Always," I reply, and spread my legs.

EPILOGUE

Harper:

Three months later...

The rainy season is finally over. For the last three months, we've waited impatiently for the weather to clear, and now, it's time to move out of our camp in the Na'Lung Cliffs, and back to the lowlands. It's time to go in search of the Cloakship, if it indeed exists, and it's time to rescue the other women.

Olivia, May, Paige, Felicity, and Bryce, we're coming for you. Hang tight.

But I'm getting ahead of myself.

The day after Beirax tried to take me hostage, Arax consulted with Viola, Ryanna, Sofia, and I. "Beirax caused injury to the four of you when he crashed your spaceship on the prison planet," he said. "His actions led to the death of one of your companions. He tried to hurt Harper. Zorahn law dictates that the victims of Beirax's crimes may determine his punishment."

"That's us?" I'd asked, stunned.

He'd nodded grimly.

"How the hell are we supposed to decide what to do with him?" Viola had demanded. "I mean, I don't like Beirax, but I don't want him to die." She'd turned to me. "Do you?"

I'm not going to lie. Part of me wanted to pass a death-sentence on the Zorahn. Not because of what he did to me, but because of what he was planning to do with my mates. He knew that their wings would be seriously damaged if they flew in the rain, and he hadn't cared. He'd demonstrated that he didn't think of any of us as people, just pawns on his chessboard.

And yet, I didn't want his death on my conscience.

"You can ask for advice, you know," Vulrux had said at my side, his lips curling up into a smile.

"We can?"

"Of course."

We'd talked for hours, trying to figure out what to do with the man. Finally, it was Nyx that had come up with the solution. "Exile him," he'd said. "You know the Dsar Cliffs, the ones we've never been able to climb because the ascent is too steep? We could fly him to the top of it and leave him there."

"We can't starve him," Sofia had protested immediately, her expression horrified.

"We won't," Dennox had replied. "We'll take him food and water." He'd looked thoughtful. "The only way to reach the peak of the Dsar Cliffs is to fly," he'd said. "It's a very effective, very isolated prison."

"In that case, that's my vote," I'd said promptly.

After that, it was Raiht'vi's turn. I'd braced myself for a death sentence, convinced that Vulrux and Dennox would want to avenge their first mate, but I was wrong.

Dennox spoke first. "I remember you," he'd said to Raiht'vi. "You were just a child when they brought you underground. You were frightened the first day. Terrified about what was happening."

"I was fifteen," she'd replied, her voice steady, her gaze never wavering from his face. "I don't need your pity, soldier. I was old enough to know what I did."

"I killed my first man when I was fifteen," Dennox had replied quietly. "He was a slaver, and deserved to die, but my heart ached for days after, remembering the look of surprise on his face as he clutched the wound in his abdomen. I forgot many things, but that image never left me. This isn't pity, scientist. This is understanding." He'd turned to Arax. "We all had fresh starts on the prison planet," he'd said. "Raiht'vi deserves one too."

"You saved Harper's life," Vulrux had added. "And for that, Raiht'vi, you will always have my gratitude. I agree with Dennox."

Arax had frowned. "You are welcome to live with us, Raiht'vi," he'd said, and then his voice had hardened. "My cousin and his pair-bond forgive you. I'm more cautious. If you harm us in any way, there will be consequences."

Which brings us to the present day. Arax and Nyx are going to fly Beirax to his mountaintop prison, and then we're dividing into two groups.

Arax, Nyx, Viola, Rorix, Ferix, and Sofia are going to look for the Draekons that took the other women.

Thrax, Zorux, and Ryanna are accompanying Vulrux, Dennox, and me in the search for the cloakship.

And if we find a way out of the prison planet, what happens next?

I don't know.

The three of us have talked about it. We can't go back to Zoraht—their fear and prejudice against Draekons are too great. We can't go back to Earth—can you imagine a shape-shifting dragon in the middle of LA? That'll create one hell of a traffic jam, and the highways are clogged enough, thank you very much.

Confession: I don't even know if I want to leave. The prison planet might not have Starbucks, but I'm starting to get very fond of it. It is the place where I fell in love with my mates, after all.

But if we do want to go, there's a whole galaxy out there. As long as Dennox and Vulrux are with me, I can be happy anywhere.

Whatever the future holds, I'm ready. *Bring it on.*

THANK you for reading Draekon Fire!

The prison planet adventures continue in Draekon Heart, Ryanna, Thrax and Zorux's story. Keep reading for a preview, or click here to purchase it.

There might be a way out of the prison planet. The only problem? I don't want to go.

Back on Earth is a man who wants to kill me.
Back on Earth, I slept with a knife under my pillow to be safe.

There's no coffee on the prison planet. No pizza. No chocolate.
I should be thrilled that there might be a way back home.
Except I don't want to return.

Here, I feel safe.
Because Mike isn't here.
And because Thrax and Zorux are.

But I've sworn off guys.
No matter how hot they are.
No matter how much I want to kiss them.
No matter how much I want to run my hands all over their hard bodies...

LEE

SAV

INO

L

ILI

Z

ANDER

Because there are a hundred reasons why the three of us shouldn't be together.
There's still no sign of my friends.
The rescue attempt is spiralling into disaster.
And most importantly, I'm fairly sure that the Draekons I'm falling in love with aren't my mates.

Draekon Heart is the third book in the Dragons in Exile series. It's a full-length, standalone science fiction dragon-shifter MFM menage romance story featuring a wary human female, and two sexy aliens that win her trust and her heart. (No M/M) Happily-ever-after guaranteed!

One-click DRAEKON HEART now!

∾

Are you all caught up with the Draekons? Don't miss any of the books.

Draekon Mate - Viola's story
Draekon Fire - Harper's story
Draekon Heart - Ryanna's story
Draekon Abduction - Olivia's story
Draekon Destiny - Felicity's story
Daughter of Draekons - Harper's birth story
Draekon Fever - Sofia's story
Draekon Rogue - Bryce's story
Draekon Holiday - A holiday story

∾

The **Must Love Draekons** newsletter is your source for all things Draekon. Subscribe today and receive a free copy of Draekon Rescue, a special Draekon story not available for sale.

A PREVIEW OF DRAEKON HEART

CHAPTER 1

Ryanna:

The dining hall in the Draekon camp is normally a place of laughter and conversation, a place where we relax after a long day of work.

Today, it's deathly silent.

All eyes are on the man who kneels in the middle of the hall, his hands tied behind his back. Beirax.

There's an expectant hush in the air.

I look around discreetly. There's something almost savage in the expressions of the Draekons as they wait for the sentencing. The scientists of Zorahn were responsible for their exile to this planet. Beirax's trial won't change their past or the reality of their harsh existence, but they still want to see him punished.

This sentencing is a formality—Beirax's punishment has been determined behind closed doors. Even though I know that, when I see the raw emotion on the faces of the Draekons, a shiver goes up my spine.

The only Draekon who holds himself apart from the others is Zorux. The powerfully-built man stands outside the circle, leaning against a pillar, wearing his customary frown. He talks to no one and no one talks to him. That's not new. Surly Draekon, as I've nicknamed him, keeps himself apart and avoids the others as much as he can.

Fine by me. I got my fill of jerks with mercurial mood swings back on Earth. I've learned my lesson.

It's easy to lose track of time on a planet where there are no clocks, but I think I've been here for three months. In that time, I've gone all 'Swiss Family Robinson' on this planet's ass—chopping wood, sharpening axes, and mending roofs. Surly Draekon—Zorux—has taught me to throw knives so I may hunt in the dry season. (Not by choice, of course; Arax told him to.) I've learned how to make a fire. I've been taught which strange alien vegetables and fruits are edible, and which ones are poisonous.

A movement distracts me from my thoughts. Thrax saunters up to the others, an easy smile on his face. God, his ass is *fine*. I have to remind myself to keep my gaze on his face. Not that looking into his caramel brown eyes is a hardship either.

Looking is okay. Touching, on the other hand, is *strictly* off-limits. Long before I left Earth, I'd made myself a promise. No more men. The more handsome they are, the more I'm going to avoid them.

I didn't realize an alien prison planet would hold so much temptation.

Forcing myself not to stare at the tall, bronzed, handsome alien, I resume my study of the people around me. Raiht'vi is expressionless. Viola's expression is carefully neutral as well, though she's gripping Nyx's hand tightly. She's not as composed as she pretends to be. Sofia looks openly distressed, and Harper is pale-faced and looks like she's going to be sick.

I don't blame them for their nerves. The four of us have a role in today's trial, and none of us are looking forward to it.

A deep gong sounds. Arax and Vulrux walk out from a house in the clearing and make their way toward us. They're dressed in strange, unfamiliar robes that cover their bodies from head to toe. The robes are golden in hue, and the fabric shimmers as they move. Around their necks are heavy, carved medallions. Thin metal bands circle their foreheads.

Back on Zoraht, Arax and Vulrux were royalty. These must be marks of their office.

The two men enter the hall and the waiting Draekons part. Beirax looks up as they approach, his expression defiant. "You are Draekon," he spits out. "You have no right to the symbols of the Crystal Throne."

"The same Crystal Throne that you and your friends are plotting to overthrow," Vulrux remarks scathingly.

"Enough." Arax's voice is quiet, but it carries through the dining hall. He eyes Beirax with unconcealed loathing. "Beirax. Your reckless actions resulted in the death of the human woman, Janet Cane. Because of you, nine other women are marooned on the prison planet, forced to live a life they didn't choose. Furthermore, in a bid to escape from your judgment, you kidnapped Harper Boyd and tried to hurt her."

Hisses sound in the crowd. Arax continues, the words formal and ritualistic. "We are here today to pass sentence on Beirax und Kronox ab Kei." His gaze rests on Viola.

"Viola Lewis. You have been injured by the actions of this man. By the laws of our land, you may choose his punishment. Do you condemn him to death?"

Viola draws a breath, but before she can speak, Beirax lunges to his feet. "No," he shouts. "Stop this farce. You are all exiles, stripped of your titles, your blood status, your possessions. You are nothing. You have no right to pass judgment on me."

I snort inwardly. I didn't hear Beirax protest when Vulrux healed him of his wounds. Funny how that works.

Arax's eyes flash with fury. The bronzed scales on his skin grow more prominent as his dragon threatens to surface. Straightening to his full height, he looks around at his fellow Draekons. "I am Arax und Dravex ab Zoraht, Firstborn of the High Empire. Does anyone here deny me the right to speak?"

Beirax's eyes swing to Raiht'vi, his expression hopeful, but she shakes her head. Nobody else speaks up.

"I am far from home," Arax says to Beirax. "And I might never return to the homeworld. But," his expression turns icy, "I will always enforce the laws of my people." He turns to Viola. "What is your answer, Viola Lewis?"

"No," she replies. Her voice is unsteady, and Nyx puts his arm around her shoulders for support. "The four of us have conferred. We do not want Beirax's death on our consciences."

The Draekons stir restlessly as Beirax slumps with relief, but we're not done. "Very well," Arax says. "Your wishes will be respected." He eyes the prisoner with distaste. "My mate is more merciful than I am. Beirax, as punishment for your many crimes, you will spend the rest of your days imprisoned on the Dsar Cliffs."

For some reason, my gaze falls on Zorux. His face has

turned pale, and he clutches the pillar for support. I wonder why Surly Draekon is freaking out.

Zorux:

I will always enforce the laws of my people.

The Firstborn's words echo in my head, over and over, until my vision blurs and my throat clogs with fear. Beirax is right; we are all exiles. Zorahn laws should not apply to the prison planet, but yet they do, *and I have broken the most important law of them all.*

On the homeworld, the tattoos on your body tell a story of who you are.

My skin is covered with ink. Twenty thin rings around my forearm mark the twenty times I passed the Testing. My chest is marked with the indigo swirls that denote my place in Zorahn society.

According to the markings, I am Zorux und Saarex ab Rykiel, Highborn of Zoraht. My ancestral home is in Ryki, the remote farming outpost in the middle of the Northern Wilds. There, the House of Rykiel has controlled the supply of the *lyka* spice for thousands of years.

But the markings are a lie. Ninety-five years ago, my father, Kavax, a Lowborn servant of Lord Saarex, killed his master and bribed a calligrapher to sear off the tattoos on his skin and replace them with those of Lord Saarex's.

Ryki was in the middle of nowhere; Lord Saarex suffered from a debilitating illness and hadn't been seen in public for over a decade. My father got away with it.

Impersonating a Highborn is one of the high crimes of the Empire. The punishment is death, not just to the person who committed the crime, but to his entire family. The bloodline is tainted and must be eliminated.

After four years, my father married my mother Lil'vi, a Highborn woman from Giflan. They had five children. My oldest sister Kael'vi. Me. The twins, Daerix and Kaenix, and my baby sister Sila'vi.

Then, when I was ten, my father was injured in a hunting accident. At the point of death, delirious from the healer's potions, he confessed the truth to my mother.

At which time Lil'vi took the ceremonial dagger of the House of Rykiel from the armory where it was stored. She slit my father's throat first. Then she killed my twelve-year-old sister Kael'vi. I would have been next, but my father's dying cries woke me. I shielded my siblings from the knife, and the blade slashed across my face, leaving a long, jagged cut.

Before she took her own life, my mother commanded me to kill my brothers and sister and cleanse the taint. Then she plunged the blade into her chest and breathed her last.

I will always enforce the laws of my people.

For sixty years, I've kept my guard up. I cannot trust anyone with this dark secret. My mother killed her own child in shame. If the Firstborn finds out what my family did, my life is forfeit.

We head out tomorrow in search of a cloakship. If there is truly a way to escape the prison planet, the danger has increased a hundred-fold. It is not my death that I fear. It is the deaths of Daerix, Kaenix, and Sila'vi.

I will always enforce the laws of my people.

If the truth is exposed, my siblings will be executed.

∾

CHAPTER 2

Thrax:

After Beirax is led away, Arax claps for attention. "I need to talk to some people," he says. "Nyx, Vulrux, Dennox, Thrax, and Zorux." He hesitates for a second and then seems to make up his mind about something. "Raiht'vi as well. If the rest of you could give us some privacy?" It's worded as a request, and everyone immediately obeys. In a few minutes, the dining area has emptied out of everyone but us.

The human women stay seated. Arax's eyes rest of his mate Viola, who's looking determined. "I'm just going to come looking for you if you leave me behind," she says. "You might as well let me tag along, and you know it."

Arax gives his mate a fondly exasperated look. "I wasn't even going to try. I knew better. If all human women are this stubborn," he adds ruefully, "I pity the men on your planet."

Harper laughs out loud, but my gaze isn't on her. My eyes are drawn instead to the human woman, Ryanna Dickson.

Before I was exiled, I never lacked for female company. I was a pilot, after all. But every woman that shared my bed knew that I wasn't looking for anything more than a night or two. I never felt a desire to stick around. There was always another planet to explore.

Sixty years on the prison planet has made me see life through a different, more patient lens. I haven't changed as much as I've grown up. I've learned to appreciate the important things in life.

Like Ryanna.

The human woman is intriguing, fascinating, and filled with contradictions. I'm not vain; I can tell when someone's attracted to me, and Ryanna clearly is. Yet, though I flirt with her, I've made no serious attempt to get her in my bed.

She's cheerful and optimistic. She's always available to lend a hand. Some of the other human women will talk about aspects of their lives back on Earth, but never Ryanna. I don't understand why, but she almost seems happy to be marooned on the prison planet.

The truth is, she's the kind of woman that deserves a man that sticks around, and that isn't me.

The Firstborn clears his throat, and everyone stops talking. "As you all know," he begins, "tomorrow, we embark on two dangerous journeys. The first, which Nyx and I will lead, is the search for the human women that were taken from *Fehrat 1*. Vulrux and Dennox will lead the second mission, the search for the Cloakship pieces."

Vulrux leans forward, a frown on his face. "I don't like this plan," he says bluntly. "Five human women were taken by the other exile batch. By now, ten Draekons might be able to transform at will. Don't be reckless, Arax. There's no hurry to find the Cloakship. Dennox and I should come with you."

"Unfortunately, it can't wait." Arax takes a deep breath. "We can't risk someone else finding the Cloakship before us. If the same Exile batch that took the human women manage to assemble the ship..." His voice trails off.

Ryanna goes pale with worry for her friends. I fight the urge to put my arms around her and comfort her. Arax continues speaking. "Beirax's supplies are in a part of the planet that we've never explored. Harper and Ryanna, I'd feel much better if the two of you would stay in the safety of this camp."

He's absolutely right. The two women are too precious to

be risked in this foolhardy trip. Especially Ryanna, who doesn't possess the Draekon mutation.

Across from me, Zorux nods in agreement. "The Lowlands are dangerous for humans."

That might be the first time I've ever seen eye-to-eye with him. Of course, Ryanna doesn't listen. "Well, I'm going," she says firmly. "There's nothing y'all can say that's going to change my mind."

"Me neither," Harper says firmly.

"That's what I thought you'd say." Vulrux looks resigned. I notice he isn't even trying to keep his mate from accompanying him. "That's why I'd like Thrax and Zorux to accompany us. Thrax used to be a pilot, so if we find the Cloakship, he'll be useful. And Zorux is pretty handy in a fight."

Arax nods in agreement. Raiht'vi, who's been silent up to this point speaks up. "Why did you ask me here? This rescue mission does not concern me."

I lift my head and stare at the scientist. Arax gives her a hard look. "I know you don't care about the humans," he snaps. "But I thought you'd be interested in the Cloakship. After all, it represents a way back to the homeworld. Don't you want to return?"

She stares back at him, unfazed. "Only a trained pilot with Draekon reflexes can fly a ship through the asteroid belt," she replies dismissively.

"You were piloting *Fehrat 1*," Ryanna says. "You know how to fly a ship."

"I'm Zorahn, human," she says. Her dismissive tone grates at me. Ryanna's statement was perfectly logical, and there's no need for the scientist to act condescending. "I don't carry the mutation in my blood. My reflexes are not fast enough." Her gaze rests on me. "Your only pilot has not transformed," she says. "Until he does, there's no way off this planet. You're embarking on a fool's errand."

"Nonetheless," Arax says coolly, "my mind is made up. I don't trust you enough to leave you behind. You're going with Vulrux."

~

Ryanna:

My heart sinks. Vulrux, Dennox, and Harper are in the *fuck-like-bunnies* stage of their relationship, which means I'll be spending a lot of time with Sexy Draekon and Surly Draekon. Great.

I take a deep breath and focus on what's important. *I'm not on Earth. Mike can't get me here. I'm safe on the prison planet.*

I set off toward the house I'm sharing with Sofia. "Ryanna, wait up," Harper says, bounding to my side. "So this should be interesting," she says. "You, me, the guys, and Raiht'vi." She raises her eyebrows as she mentions the scientist. "Is it just me, or does the way she says the word 'human' sound like an insult?"

I giggle, picturing the arrogant Zorahn. "Definitely not just you. I'm pretty sure she thinks we're one evolutionary step above pond scum, bless her heart."

Harper cackles. "This is why I love you, Ryanna. You're so nice, and everything you say sounds so sweet in that Georgian accent of yours. But whenever you say 'bless your heart' I hear something else." She winks at me.

"Don't tell anyone." I grin back at her. "My grandma used to say 'bless your heart' is Southern for 'fuck you.'"

"Wouldn't dream of it. All these Draekons think you're a peach."

"If they knew what a peach was." I swallow as homesickness hits me hard.

"Yeah." Harper sobers up. "You think this mission will work?"

"I don't know."

"Hey, at least you'll get to hang with Thrax. What?" She shrugs when I stare at her. "I see the way you look at him. He's cute. You should go for it."

I stiffen. "No," I say a little too sharply. "I mean... before I left, I had a bad breakup."

More like a bad break. My arm, in three places, not to mention the bruises and a black eye.

"I'm sorry." She pats my arm, an understanding expression on her face.

"It's fine," I shrug, wanting to change the topic. I don't like talking about what happened back home.

Harper heads off to the house she shares with her mates. I'm not jealous, not exactly. Sure, I notice the way Vulrux and Dennox look at her, but when I imagine a man looking at me the same way... my stomach tightens. A loving look, a gentle touch—they all lead to darker memories. I'm never going down that road again. No matter how cute I think Thrax is.

Footsteps behind me make me whirl. I sigh in relief as Thrax falls into place at my side. The Draekon is almost two feet taller than me and ripped like a prize fighter, but I've never felt threatened by him. "You're determined to come with us, aren't you?" he asks me unhappily.

I will not live my life in fear.

"Are you going to try and talk me out of it?" In the time I've known him, Thrax has always treated me as if I were strong and capable. He's never acted as if I was a liability. For him to try to dissuade me from this mission...

"Zorux is right. The Lowlands are dangerous."

I'm used to living in a state of constant terror. No matter how dangerous the Lowlands are, I feel safer on the prison planet, scary predators and all, than I did back home in Georgia. "I'm not helpless," I say quietly, trying to convince myself as much as him.

Without meaning to, I've scooted closer to him as we walk. The Draekon even smells good. A little smoky, like bourbon or tobacco. The scent reminds me the evenings my grandpa sat on the porch smoking his pipe. One of my better memories of Earth, of a time I was loved and safe.

He gives me a warm smile. "Not at all," he agrees. "Your first day here, you faced down a trio of Dwals and shot two of them. You saved Sofia and Harper's lives. How can anyone think of you as helpless?"

He's right. *I did do that.* I smile at him, grateful for the words of support. "Thank you, Thrax."

Goodbye, nice and safe Draekon camp.

Hello, crazy jungle world.

I'm ready for you.

~

Click here to keep reading Draekon Heart, book 3 of the **Dragons in Exile** series. The book is a standalone MFM menage romance with a guaranteed HEA!

ABOUT THE AUTHORS

Lili Zander is the sci-fi romance loving alter-ego of Tara Crescent. She lives in Toronto. She enjoys reading sci-fi and fantasy, and thinks a great romance makes every book better.

Find Lili at:
www.lilizander.com
www.facebook.com/authorlilizander
Email her at lili@lilizander.com

Lee Savino is a USA today bestselling author. She's also a mom and a choco-holic. She's written a bunch of books—all of them are "smexy" romance. Smexy, as in "smart and sexy."

Download a free book from www.leesavino.com.

Find Lee at:
www.leesavino.com
www.facebook.com/leesavinoauthor

BOOKS BY LILI ZANDER

The Alien Vampires of Shayde (Vampires in space, reverse harem)

Night of the Shayde

Blood of the Shayde - *coming Spring 2019*

Blood Prophecy (Dragon shifters, reverse harem)

Dragon's Thief

Dragon's Curse

Dragon's Hope

Dragon's Ruin

Dragon's Treasure

or

Dragon's Fire (the omnibus edition, containing all the Blood Prophecy episodes) *and a bonus story,* Dragon's Ghost.

Adventures of Suzie and the Alien

BOOKS BY LEE SAVINO

Hey there. It's me, Lee Savino, your fearless author of smexy, smexy romance (smart + sexy). I'm glad you read this book. If you're like me, you're wondering what to read next. Let me help you out...

If you haven't visited my website...seriously, go sign up for the free Berserker book. It puts you on my awesome sauce email list and I send out stuff all the time via email that you can't get anywhere else. ;) leesavino.com

Then check out...

My **Berserker series**: These huge, dominant shifter warriors will stop at nothing to claim the women who can free them from the Berserker curse These books are based on an Old Norse poem I studied in college, but writing heroines who find freedom in their sexual desires is my therapy after years of religious repression. They're...ahem...quite kinky, so stay away if you don't want a fair bit of BDSM.

The series is broken into two, all set in the same world and time period:

The Berserker Saga
Berserker Brides

Then I have a few series with cowriters! Yay!

The Draekon series with Lili Zander
The Tsenturion Masters with Golden Angel
The Bad Boy Alpha series with Renee Rose

Contemporary Romance. Check out Her Marine Daddy-free on all sites except Amazon (until they decide to make it free for me). More contemporary romance books coming soon!

Printed in Great Britain
by Amazon

25241684R00108